# THE LION OF
# BOAZ-JACHIN
# AND
# JACHIN-BOAZ

*by the same author*

THE MOUSE AND HIS CHILD

# THE LION OF BOAZ-JACHIN AND JACHIN-BOAZ

## AND

# JACHIN-BOAZ

*Russell Hoban*

JONATHAN CAPE
THIRTY BEDFORD SQUARE LONDON

FIRST PUBLISHED 1973
© 1973 BY YANKEE ROVER, INC.

JONATHAN CAPE LTD
30 BEDFORD SQUARE, LONDON WCI

ISBN 0 224 00831 5

The quotation at the foot of page 132, 'It must die because it has had children and is no longer needed,' is based on a line from *The Great Chain of Life* by Joseph Wood Krutch (Houghton Mifflin Co., Cambridge, Mass., 1956): 'Volvox must die as Leeuwenhoek saw it die because it has had children and is no longer needed.' The quotation on page 176, lines 7–10, is taken from Wordsworth's 'A Slumber did my Spirit Seal'.

PRINTED IN GREAT BRITAIN
BY EBENEZER BAYLIS & SON LTD
THE TRINITY PRESS, WORCESTER, AND LONDON
ON PAPER SUPPLIED BY P. F. BINGHAM LTD
BOUND BY JAMES BURN AND CO. LTD, ESHER, SURREY

TO GUNDEL

Thou huntest me as a fierce lion:
and again thou shewest thyself
marvellous upon me.

Job x : 16

# I

There were no lions any more. There had been lions once. Sometimes in the shimmer of the heat on the plains the motion of their running still flickered on the dry wind — tawny, great, and quickly gone. Sometimes the honey-coloured moon shivered to the silence of a ghost-roar on the rising air.

There were no chariots any more. The chariots, wind-bereft and roadless in the night, slept with their tall wheels hushed in the tomb of the last king.

The ruins of the king's palace had been dug out of the ground. There was a chain-link fence all around the citadel where the palace buildings, the courtyards, the temples and the tombs had been excavated. There were a souvenir shop and a refreshment stand near the gates.

The columns and the roof beams, fallen and termite-hollowed, had been labelled and cleared away. Jackals hunted among them no more. Where snakes and lizards had sunned themselves the daylight came through the skylights in the roof of the new building that enclosed the great hall where the hunting of the king was carved in stone.

The images of horses and men, chariots and lions, were stained by weather, worn by rain, pocked and pitted by the dust that had stung them when the dry wind howled. New walls were around them now, a new roof was over them. The temperature was controlled by a thermostat. An air-conditioner made a whirring silence.

Jachin-Boaz had a wife and a son, and he lived in a town far from the sea. Pigeons flew up from the square, circled above it, and came down to perch on clay walls, red roof-tiles. The fountain sent up a slim silver jet among old women in black. The dogs knew where everything was, and went through the alleyways behind the shops like businessmen. The cats looked down from high places, disappeared around corners. Many of the women did their washing in stone sinks near the town pump. Tourists going through the town in buses looked out through the windows at the merchants who sold brass and ivory and rugs drinking coffee in the shade of awnings. The vendors of fruit and vegetables smoked in the street.

Jachin-Boaz traded in maps. He bought and sold maps, and some, of certain kinds for special uses, he made or had others make for him. That had been his father's trade, and the walls of the shop that had been his father's were hung with glazed blue oceans, green swamps and grasslands, brown and orange mountains delicately shaded. Maps of towns and plains he sold, and other maps made to order. He would sell a young man a map that showed where a particular girl might be found at different hours of the day. He sold husband maps and wife maps. He sold maps to poets that showed where thoughts of power and clarity had come to other poets. He sold well-digging maps. He sold vision-and-miracle maps to holy men, sickness-and-accident maps to physicians, money-and-jewel maps to thieves, and thief maps to the police.

Jachin-Boaz was at the age called middle life, but he did not believe that he had as many years ahead of him as he had behind him. He had married very young, and he had now been married for more than a quarter of a century. Often he was impotent with his wife. On Sundays, when the shop was closed and he was alone with her and his son through the long afternoon, he tried to shut out of his mind a lifelong despair. Often he thought of death, of himself gone and the great dark shoulder of the world for ever turning away from the nothingness of him for ever in the blackness. Lying beside his sleeping wife he would twist away from his death-thought, open-eyed and grimacing in the darkness of the bedroom over the shop. Often he dreamed of his dead mother and father while sleeping in their bed, but very seldom could he remember his dreams.

Sometimes Jachin-Boaz sat alone in the shop late at night. The green-shaded lamp on his desk threw his shadow on the maps behind him on the wall. He felt the silent waiting of all the seeking and finding that lived in the maps hung on the walls, stacked in the drawers of the cabinets. He would close his eyes, seeing clear lines in different colours that marked the migratory paths of fish and animals, winds and ocean currents, journeys to hidden sources of wisdom, passes through mountains to lodes of precious metals, secret ways through city streets to secret pleasures.

Behind his closed eyes he saw the map of his town in which the square, the town pump, the stone laundry sinks, the street of the merchants and he himself were fixed and permanent. Then he would rise from his desk and walk up and down in the dark shop, touching maps with his fingers and sighing.

Jachin-Boaz had for a number of years been working on a map for his son. From the many different maps that passed through his hands, from the reports of his information-gatherers and surveyors, from the books and journals that he read, from his own records and observations, he compiled a great body of detailed knowledge, and that knowledge was incorporated in the map for his son. He added to it con-stantly, revising and making the necessary corrections to keep it always current.

Jachin-Boaz had said nothing about the map to his wife or his son, but he spent most of his spare time on it. He did not think that his son would follow him in the shop, nor did he want him to. He wanted his son to go out into the world, and he wanted him to find more of a world for himself than he, Jachin-Boaz, had found. He had put aside some money for the boy's inheritance, but the map was to be the larger part of his legacy. It was to be nothing less than a master map that would show him where to find whatever he might wish to look for, and so would assure him of a proper start in life as a man.

The son of Jachin-Boaz was named Boaz-Jachin. When he became sixteen years old his father decided that he would show him the master map.

'Everyone in the world is looking for something,' said Jachin-Boaz to Boaz-Jachin, 'and by means of maps each thing that is found is never lost again. Centuries of finding are on the walls and in the cabinets of this shop.'

'If everything that is found is never lost again, there will be an end to finding some day,' said Boaz-Jachin. 'Some day there will be nothing left to find.' He looked more like his mother than like his father. His face was mysterious to his father, who felt that if he tried to guess his son's thoughts he would be wrong more often than not.

'That is the sort of thing that young people like to say to annoy their elders,' said Jachin-Boaz. 'Obviously there are always new things to find. And as to what has already been found, would you prefer that all knowledge be thrown away so that you might be ignorant and the world new? Is that what they teach you at school?'

'No,' said Boaz-Jachin.

'I am glad to hear that,' said Jachin-Boaz, 'because the past is the father of the present, just as I am your father. And if the past cannot teach the present and the father cannot teach the son, then history need not have bothered to go on, and the world has wasted a great deal of time.'

Boaz-Jachin looked at the maps on the walls. 'The past is not here,' he said. 'There is only the present, in which are things left behind by the past.'

'And those things are part of the present,' said Jachin-Boaz, 'and therefore to be used by the present. Look,' he said, 'this is exactly what I mean.' He took the master-map out of a drawer and spread it on the counter for his son to look at. 'I have been working on it for years,' said Jachin-Boaz, 'and it will be yours when you are a man. Everything that you could wish to look for is on this map. I take great pains to keep it up to date, and I add to it all the time.'

Boaz-Jachin looked at the map, at the cities and towns, the blue oceans, the green swamps and grasslands, the delicately shaded brown and orange mountains, the clear lines in inks of different colours that showed where all things known to his father might be found by him. He looked away from the map and down at the floor.

'What do you think of it?' said Jachin-Boaz.

Boaz-Jachin said nothing.

'Why won't you say anything?' said his father. 'Look at this labour of years, with everything clearly marked upon it. This map represents not only the years of my life spent upon it, but the years of other lives spent in gathering the information that is here. What can you seek that this map will not show you how to find?'

Boaz-Jachin looked at the map, then at his father. He looked all around the shop and down at his feet, but he said nothing.

'Please don't stand there saying nothing,' said Jachin-Boaz. 'Say something. Name something that this map will not show you how to find.'

Boaz-Jachin looked around the shop again. He looked at the iron door-stop. It was in the shape of a crouching lion. He looked at his father with a half-smile. 'A lion?' he said.

'A lion,' said Jachin-Boaz. 'I don't think I understand you. I don't think you're being serious with me. You know very well there are no lions now. The wild ones were hunted to extinction. Those in captivity were killed off by a disease that travelled from one country to another carried by fleas. I don't know what kind of a joke that was meant to be.' As he spoke there opened in his mind great mystical amber eyes, luminous and infinite. There blossomed great taloned paws, heavy and powerful. There was a silent roar, round, endless, an orb of reflection imaging a pink rasping tongue, white teeth of death. Jachin-Boaz shook his head. There were no lions any more.

'I wasn't making a joke,' said Boaz-Jachin. 'I was looking at the door-stop and I thought of lions.'

Jachin-Boaz nodded his head, put the map back into its drawer, went to the back of the shop and sat down at his desk.

Boaz-Jachin went to his room on the top floor over the shop. He looked out through the window at the clear twilight, the darkening red-tiled roofs and the tops of the palm trees around the square.

Then he sat down and played his guitar. The room grew dark around him, and for a time he played in the dim light that came from the lamps in the street. Not here, said the guitar to the walls of the room. Beyond here.

Boaz-Jachin put away his guitar and lit the lamp on his desk. From a drawer he took a sheet of paper on which was a roughly sketched map. Many of the lines had been erased and drawn over. The paper was dirty and the map seemed empty compared to the one that his father had shown him. He began to draw a line very lightly from one point to another. Then he erased the line and put the map away. He turned out the light, lay on his bed, looked at the lamplight from the street on the ceiling and listened to the pigeons on the roof.

# 2

Jachin-Boaz dreamed every night, and every morning he forgot his dreams. One night he dreamed of the scissorman his mother had told him about when he was a child. The scissorman punished boys who wet their beds by cutting off their noses. Had she said noses? In Jachin-Boaz's dream the scissorman was huge, dressed all in black, with great hunched shoulders, a long red nose, and a beard like that of his father. Jachin-Boaz had done something terribly bad, and he was to have his arms and legs cut off by the dreadful scissors. 'It won't hurt very much at all,' said the scissorman. 'Actually it will be a great relief for you to be rid of those heavy members – they're really too much for you to carry around.' When he cut off Jachin-Boaz's left arm the scissors sounded as if they were cutting paper, and there was no pain. But Jachin-Boaz cried 'No!' and woke up with his heart pounding. Then he went back to sleep. In the morning he had not forgotten the dream. His wife was in the kitchen making breakfast, and he sat on the edge of the bed trying to remember how many years ago he had stopped waking up with an erection. He could not remember when it had happened last.

A few months later Jachin-Boaz said that he was going on a field trip for several weeks. He packed his map-case, his drawing instruments, his compass and binoculars and the rest of his field gear. He said that he was meeting a surveyor in the next town and that they were going to travel inland. Then he took a train to the seaport.

A month passed, and Jachin-Boaz did not return. Boaz-

Jachin opened the drawer where the master-map was kept. It was not there. In the drawer were the deed to the house and a bank-book. The house and the savings account had been transferred to Jachin-Boaz's wife. Half of the savings had been withdrawn. There was a note in the drawer:

I have gone to look for a lion.

'What does he mean by that?' said Jachin-Boaz's wife. 'Has he gone mad? There are no lions to be found.'

'He's not looking for a lion of *that* shape,' said Boaz-Jachin, indicating the door-stop. 'He means something else. And he's taken the map that he said he would give me.'

'He's taken half of our savings,' said his mother.

'If we lived without using the savings before,' said Boaz-Jachin, 'we can live without the half that he has taken.'

Boaz-Jachin and his mother took on the management of the shop, and in the hours when he was not at school Boaz-Jachin sold maps and worked on the special orders with surveyors, information-gatherers and draughtsmen. He, like his father, came to know of the many things that people were looking for and the places where they could be found. Often he thought of the master-map that had been promised him.

I sit in the shop like an old man, selling maps to help other people find things, thought Boaz-Jachin, because my father has taken my map for himself and has run off to find a new life with it. The boy has become an old man and the old man has become a boy.

Boaz-Jachin took his old sketch-map from the drawer of his desk and began to work on it again. He spoke to the information-gatherers and surveyors, and he wrote in a notebook whatever seemed useful. He walked the streets and alleyways of the town late at night and early in the morning. He learned more and more about what people

16

were looking for and where they found it. Boaz-Jachin worked hard on his map, but it still looked empty and confused compared to the one that his father had shown him. His lines were dirty and straggling, and lacked the pattern of intelligent purpose. The routes shown in his father's map had had a clarity and logic that made his own efforts seem poor. He was uncertain of what to seek, and he had little confidence in his ability to find anything. He told one of the surveyors of his difficulties.

'For years I have sighted and measured and located this point and that point on the face of the earth,' said the surveyor, 'and I have gone back to the same places to find my stakes pulled out as boundaries waver and lose accuracy. I sight and I measure and I plant the stakes again, knowing they will be pulled out again. It is not only stakes and boundaries that are lost—this is what there is to know about maps, and I tell you what I have paid years to learn: everything that is found is always lost again, and nothing that is found is ever lost again. Can you understand that? You're still a boy, so maybe you can't. Can you understand that?'

Boaz-Jachin thought about the surveyor's words. He understood the words, but the meaning of them did not enter him because their meaning was not an answer to any question in him. In his mind he saw an oblong of blue sky edged with dark faces. He felt a roaring in him, and opened and closed his mouth silently. 'No,' he said.

'You're still a boy. You will learn,' said the surveyor.

Boaz-Jachin continued to work on his map, but without real interest. The places he had thought of going to and the routes by which he had thought to reach those places seemed foolish to him now. The more he thought about his father's master-map the more he realized that he had not been capable of judging its worth when Jachin-Boaz had shown it to him. It was not simply a matter of neatness and finish—he saw now that the scope and detail of the conception were far beyond him. That map seemed the answer to everything, and his father had taken it away from him.

Boaz-Jachin decided to find his father and ask him for the master-map. He had no idea where Jachin-Boaz might be, but he did not think that the way to find him was to attempt to trace him from town to town, village to village, and across mountains and plains. He felt that there was a place he must find first, and in that place he would know how to proceed in his search.

He walked up and down the aisles of the shop, passing and repassing the maps in the cabinets, the maps on the walls. He stood looking at the crouching iron lion doorstop. ' "I have gone to look for a lion," ' he said. There were no lions any more. There were no lion-places. 'A place of lions,' he said. 'A place of lions. A lion-place. A lion-palace.' There was a lion-palace in the desert that he had read of. There was a place where the last king lay in his tomb and his lion-hunt was carved in stone on the walls of the great hall. He looked at a map and saw that the palace was near a town that was only three hours away by bus.

That Friday afternoon Boaz-Jachin told his mother that he was going to visit a friend in another town for the weekend. She gave him some money for his travel expenses, and when she was not in the office at the back of the shop he took more money from the cash box. He packed some clothes in a rucksack, took his guitar and his unfinished map, went to the bus depot, and bought a one-way ticket.

There were boys and girls of his own age on the bus, laughing, talking, eating lunches they had brought with them, fondling one another. Boaz-Jachin looked away from them. He had a girl that he had never made love with. He had not said goodbye to her. He sat next to a fat man who smelled of shaving lotion. As the bus left the town he looked out the window at petrol stations and shacks with corrugated metal roofs. Out in the country he watched the dry brown land, the meagre hills, the passing telephone poles. Sometimes people stood waiting with cheap suitcases. Once the bus stopped to let a flock of sheep cross the road. The sky darkened until he saw only his own face in the window.

When the bus reached the town the petrol stations were bright, harshly lit, and closed. Everything else was dark except for a few cafés, yellow-and-red-lit, with a thin wail of music and a smell of stale grease. Dogs trotted through the empty streets.

The man at the ticket window in the bus station said that the palace was three miles outside the town and that the next bus would be at ten o'clock in the morning. Boaz-Jachin weighed himself, bought a chocolate bar, and walked out to the road.

The yellow lamps were far apart, with blackness in between. There was no moon. Few cars passed, and between their passing he heard the chirping of crickets and the distant barking of dogs. Boaz-Jachin did not try to get a lift, and nobody offered him one. His footsteps on the stones of the roadside sounded far away from everything.

It seemed a long time before he came to the chain-link fence around the citadel where the palace had been dug out of the desert. Not far from the locked gates he saw the fluorescent-lit window of a low building where the guards sat drinking coffee.

Boaz-Jachin threw his rucksack over the fence and heard it thump on the other side. He took off his belt, buckled it around the handle of his guitar-case, slung the case from his shoulder, climbed the fence, scraping his fingers and tearing his trousers on the wire-ends at the top, and dropped heavily to the ground on the other side.

He could see well enough in the starlight to find the building that housed the ruins of the great hall and the lion-hunt carvings. The door was unlocked, so he knew that the guards would be coming through it on their rounds. Boaz-Jachin saw skylights above him, but the inside of the building was much darker than the night outside. He carefully felt his way along. He found a cupboard that smelled of floor wax, felt mops and brooms in it. He made a space for himself on the floor so that he could sit leaning against the wall. He fell asleep.

When Boaz-Jachin woke up he looked at his watch. It was a quarter past six. He opened the cupboard door and saw daylight in the building. He walked past the carvings, not looking at them yet. He looked down at the floor until he came to the end of the hall and the corridor where the toilets were. When he had relieved himself he washed his hands and face and looked at himself in the mirror. He said his name three times: 'Boaz-Jachin, Boaz-Jachin, Boaz-Jachin.' Then he said his father's name once: 'Jachin-Boaz.'

He walked back through the hall, not looking at the walls on either side, but keeping to the middle by looking up at the skylights. When he was ready, he stopped and looked to his left.

Carved in the brownish stone was a lion with two arrows in his spine, leaping up at the king's chariot from behind, biting the tall chariot wheel, dying on the spears of the king and the king's spearmen. The horses galloped on, the beard of the calm-faced king was carefully curled, the king looked straight out over the back of the chariot, over the lion biting the wheel and dying on his spear. With both front paws the lion clung to the turning wheel that pulled him up on to the spears. His teeth were in the wheel, his muzzle was wrinkled back from his teeth, his brows were drawn together in a frown, his eyes were looking straight out from the shadow of his brows. There was no expression on the king's face. He was looking over the lion and beyond him.

'The king is nothing. Nothing, nothing, nothing,' said Boaz-Jachin. He began to cry. He ran to the cupboard, closed the door, sat down on the floor in the dark, and wept. When he had finished crying he left the building by the exit that was not visible from the guards' hut and hid behind a shed until the first bus brought sightseers whose presence allowed him to walk about freely.

Boaz-Jachin went back into the hall. Before going back to the lion he had seen first he looked quickly at the other lion-hunt reliefs. There were many lions being killed by the calm-faced king with arrows, spears, even with a sword. None of the other lions mattered to Boaz-Jachin. For a long time, while voices chattered around him and footsteps shuffled past, Boaz-Jachin looked at the dying lion biting the chariot wheel.

Then he went outside again and walked among the excavated ruins of the several palace buildings, the court-yards, the temples and the tombs. The sky was pale and hot. Everything was lion-coloured, low, tawny, broken, pre-served in forgottenness, found so that its lostness might be fixed and made permanent, fenced-in, broken-toothed, stripped naked of time and earth, humbled, refusing to say a word.

At some distance from the palace ruins a sign identified a high mound as the artificial hill on which spectators had stood while the lions, released from cages on the plain below, were hunted by the king.

Boaz-Jachin climbed the hill and sat there, looking out over the lion-coloured plain, dotted now with children and grown-ups photographing one another, eating sandwiches and drinking soft drinks. The grown-ups looked at maps of the citadel and pointed in various directions. The children spilled food and drinks on their clothes, quarrelled among themselves, ran, walked, and jumped violently and at random. Their voices rose in a thin haze like the smell of old cooking in a block of flats. The heat shimmered over the plain, and Boaz-Jachin fancied that he could see in the air the running of the lions, tawny, great, quickly gone. He felt in him the dying lion biting the wheel. By letting go of everything else he could let himself be with the lion.

And being with the lion he tasted in him, raging, the memory of the trap and the fall, the blue oblong of sky above him, the dark faces looking down into the pit, the heavy corded meshes of the net that came down over him and clung and smothered and made impotent his rage. Dark of the pit, blue of the sky, and the peering dark faces of little dark men who were outlanders everywhere, the little dark men who read the wind, who read the earth they walked on. When they hunted they looked from side to side and sniffed the air. In the invisible air that held the spirits of beasts living and dead they felt with quick strong fingers, and they pulled out like a long thread the spirit of the animal they would trap. The lion could kill them with a blow of his paw if they would stand before him, but they were too cunning. The lion was as a child to them.

The memory of the heavy cage-wagons was in Boaz-Jachin, the jolting and the dryness and the thirst. Then the wooden cages on the plain and the other little cages atop them in which the little dark cunning men perched like birds. With poles they opened the cage doors and sent the lions out in the heat of the day to the place of their death.

The lions came out of the cages slowly, snarling and lashing their tails. They crouched, growling while the beaters and their dogs advanced to make them go forward to be hunted by the king. The dry wind offered chaos only. The dry wind sang the hunter hunted, the last kill far behind.

The dry wind roared and raged, clashed spears on shields, bayed in the mastiff throats, sang in bowstrings death, death, death.

The lions were out on the plain. Beaters and dogs and spearmen and men with shields made walls they could not break through, could not overleap. The chariots were rolling on their tall wheels and the king was shooting arrows, sending death among the lions.

The lions were brave, but there was no chance for them. If they had had a king he would have led them against the king of the chariots and horses. But they had no time to choose a lion-king. The chariots were among them, with spearmen and bowmen to guard their king and give death to every lion.

The last lion alive was the one whom the others would have made their king if they had been allowed to. He was large, strong, and fierce, and with two arrows deep in his spine he was still alive. The arrows burned like fire in him, his sight was fading, the blood was roaring in his ears with the rumble of the chariot wheels. Before him and above him, racing away, the glittering king was calm in his chariot, his spear poised, his spearmen beside him. The dying lion-king leaped, clung to the tall and turning wheel that brought him up to the spears. Growling and frowning he bit the wheel that lifted him and bore him on to darkness.

The lion was gone. Where the lion had been was a sudden empty giddy blackness, like the sensation produced by straightening up too quickly after bending down for a long time.

Boaz-Jachin was aware of people again, taking photographs, eating sandwiches, drinking soft drinks. He listened for ghost-roars behind the voices, heard only the seethe of absence in the hollow of the silence, as one might hear the sea in a shell.

'There are no lions any more,' said Boaz-Jachin.

He thought about his father and the map that he had taken away. What might have been his for the finding if Jachin-Boaz had not taken the beautiful map for himself! He, son of the map-seller, map-maker, map-lover, had no talent for maps, could not make one that was not stupid and ugly and disfigured, and this was his father's way of punishing him — to leave him mapless and alone with his deserted mother, stuck in a dark shop like an old man, waiting for the bell to jingle at the door, waiting to sell the means of finding to other seekers.

Boaz-Jachin had in his rucksack, along with his clothes and his unfinished map, a pencil, some paper, and a small ruler. He went back to the hall of the lion hunt, alone among the people all around him. He measured carefully the dying lion who was leaping up at the king's chariot. He measured the visible parts of the arrows in the lion, measured also the spears of the king and the king's spearmen. In another part of the same relief was an arrow that transfixed a dying lioness. Both ends of the arrow being visible, Boaz-Jachin was able to measure its full length. He wrote down all his measurements, folded the paper carefully and put it in his pocket.

He left the lion-hunt hall and went out to the high mound, the spectator's hill. There he sat for a long time. When Boaz-Jachin had taken the money from the cash box in the office he had thought that he would not be coming back to the shop. He had seen himself, a lone wanderer, playing his guitar in the street, the case open on the pavement for passers-by to drop money into. But in the wordless refusal of the ruins about him, in the remembered sound of last night's roadside stones under his feet, he had heard the silence of unreadiness.

He had been with the lion. He had that. That had come

to him, and something had made him measure the image of the lion and the images of the spears and arrows. He did not know why he had done it. Something more might come to him. He had come to this place to find what to do next, and at least he had found what not to do next: he would not search for his father now. He would go back to the shop for the present.

At the souvenir stand near the gates Boaz-Jachin bought a photograph of the lion-hunt relief that showed the dying lion leaping up at the king's chariot and biting the turning wheel. Then he bought a sandwich and an orange drink. When the bus came he went back to the town, and from there he took the next bus back to his town.

# 3

It was late at night in the city where Jachin-Boaz lived now. He lay awake looking at the pinky-grey night sky framed in his windows. Always in the night sky here was the reflected glow of the great city. He moved his arm to light a cigarette, and the girl who lay with her head on his chest rolled over in her sleep, trailing her hand down his body. Gretel. He said her name in his mind, leaned over to look at her sleeping face, turned back the blankets to admire the graceful length of her, smiled in the dark, covered her again.

Jachin-Boaz watched the smoke drift in the dimness of the room. He thought of stories, fairy tales from his childhood, in which a young man went out to seek his fortune in the wide world. Always the father was dead at the beginning of the story, and the young man went out with his few coins, his crust of bread, his fiddle or his sword. Sometimes he found or won some magic thing along the way. A map, perhaps. Jachin-Boaz bared his teeth in the dark but did not smile.

Now he, Jachin-Boaz, was the old man out in the wide world seeking his fortune, the old man who wanted a new story and would not agree to be dead. The young man was left at home to be a shopkeeper and the companion of his deserted mother. Jachin-Boaz saw in his mind his wife's face, looked away and saw the face of his son Boaz-Jachin outside the shop window, shaded by the awning, looking into the shadows at his father and smiling.

Jachin-Boaz got out of bed. Without turning on any of the lights he walked into the next room. His desk was there, and on it lay the master-map that he had promised to his son Boaz-Jachin. By the light from the window he could see some of the routes and places marked on it.

Jachin-Boaz, naked in the dark, touched the map. 'There is only one place,' he said, 'that place is time, and that time is now. There is no other place.' He ran his fingers over the map, then turned away. The sky was lighter than before. Birds were singing.

'I never let him help me with a map,' said Jachin-Boaz. 'Sometimes he wanted to do a little of the border, but I never let him do it. He showed me little dirty maps that he had made, and he wanted praise. He wanted me to like his music, wanted me to be pleased with him, but I never said what he wanted to hear. And I left him sitting in a shop, waiting for the bell to jingle at the door.'

Jachin-Boaz went back to bed and wrapped himself around Gretel. In the mornings now he woke up with an erection.

# 4

When Boaz-Jachin came back to his town he did not go to his mother's house. This was Saturday. She would not be expecting him until Sunday evening, and he did not want to go home yet.

He called up his girl from the bus station, and went to her house. Waiting for her to come to the door he felt again the being-with-the-lion. It was a flash that came and went, full of strangeness. It made him feel apart from his regular life, apart from all the people in his mind and the girl, Lila, whom he waited for now. He felt guilty and uneasy.

The door opened. Lila looked at Boaz-Jachin's face. 'Is everything all right?' she said. 'You look strange.'

'I feel strange,' he said. 'But everything's all right.'

They walked to the square. The street lamps seemed luminous fruits, bursting with knowledge. Boaz-Jachin tasted their light in his mouth and wondered who he was. He felt strongly the ripe blackness of rooftops against the night sky, the poignancy of roofs and domes of the town fitting into the night sky. The colour and texture of the pavement, the substance of it, were intense with flavour.

He had never been naked with Lila, had never made love with her, had never done it with anyone. His orgasms had been with himself only, rumpled with shame and listening for footsteps in the hallway. He remembered his face in the mirror in the hall of the lion-hunt carvings. Who, he wondered, looked out through the eyeholes in his face?

'What are you going to do?' said Lila.

'I don't know,' he said. 'I thought I would go and look for my father. But I came back. I sat on a hill and it wasn't time yet. I was waiting for something. I don't know what I'm waiting for. I'm not ready to go yet.'

The slim jet of the fountain went up into the starlight, fell back continually. Dogs met and separated, going their separate ways. Boaz-Jachin and Lila sat on a bench. The palm trees rustled. The street lamps had not changed. His throat ached.

'I'm waiting too,' she said. 'They sit in the living room and watch television. The house feels as if it's crouching over me. On Sundays with them I'm always depressed. I don't know where to go.'

When I go, Boaz-Jachin thought, will you go with me? His throat shaped the words but he did not speak them. He thought of his going, and now the sea was in it. He had been on a ship once, on a summer holiday with his parents. 'In the middle of the ocean,' he said, 'it is green and huge and heaving, and you smell the deepness of it and the salt. Grey fog in the morning, wet on the face, cold in the stomach. The big sea-birds are never lost. They can sit down on the ocean, rocking on the waves.' When I go, will you go with me? he thought again, but again did not speak the words.

'Yes,' she said.

'Where can we go?' he said. 'Now, I mean. Where can we go now?'

'I don't know,' she said. 'Our roof. They were sitting up there after dinner, but maybe they've gone down by now. Maybe they'll be asleep by now.'

Lila and Boaz-Jachin took a blanket up to the roof. The air was warm on their naked bodies. The stars were large and brilliant. She had made love before, and she shaped herself to him, put herself where he was, made him welcome in her. He was overwhelmed by the gift. Behind his eyes everything was lion-coloured, sunlit. When the blackness came it was a roaring and an exaltation in him, a losing and a finding of himself. Afterwards he was cool, immensely easy. He was with Lila and with the lion and he was alone. He knew that when he was ready to go he would have to go alone. They slept on the roof until the sky was pale. Then Boaz-Jachin went back to his mother's house.

'It's me,' he said, hearing her wake up as he passed her door.

'Come in,' she said. 'Say hello.'

He set down the rucksack and the guitar in the hallway. They leaned against the wall. We were going away for good, they said. We came back. The smell of old cooking seemed overpowering to Boaz-Jachin. What if she gets sick and I have to take care of her? he thought. If I'd left now at least I'd have left her healthy. He went into his mother's room.

Boaz-Jachin's mother looked at her son in the dawn light in the room. 'You're home sooner than I expected,' she said. 'You look strange. What's the matter?'

'Nothing's the matter,' he said. 'I feel fine. I'm going down to the shop. I left some schoolwork there.'

Boaz-Jachin put back the money he had taken from the cash box. He heard his mother's footsteps overhead, felt a wave of hotness pass through him, then a surge of desperation. Stay here, the footsteps said. I have nothing now. Don't leave me. Boaz-Jachin ground his teeth.

When his mother came to his room later to call him for breakfast he was kneeling on a sheet of brown wrapping-paper that he had taken from the roll in the shop. The paper stretched across the full width of the floor, and he had ruled it off into large squares. On it lay the photograph of the relief of the dying lion biting the wheel. On a sheet of transparent acetate over the photograph he had ruled small squares. Now, by making what he drew in each large square on the brown paper correspond to what was in each small square on the photograph, Boaz-Jachin was developing an accurate copy that was the same size as the lion he had measured. He did not include the chariot and the king in his copy: he was drawing only the lion, the two arrows in him and the two spears at his throat that were killing him.

'What are you doing?' said his mother.

'It's for school,' said Boaz-Jachin. 'I'll be down in a minute.'

Boaz-Jachin let the being-with-the-lion come to him. He did not have to remember it — it came when he opened himself to it. He felt the lion-life, the weight and power and the surge of it like a river of violence, calm and huge. He felt the lion-life rush into the death that came on to darken it, and he was at a moving point of balance in between. He drew his lines delicately in pencil at first, then went over them firmly with a felt-tipped pen. His lines were strong and black. The brown paper was clean and unsmudged.

# 5

Gretel, who worked in a bookshop, had helped Jachin-Boaz find a job as an assistant in another shop. His salary was small and the owner was delighted with him. There was about Jachin-Boaz an aura of seeking and finding that customers responded to. People who for years had not looked for things in books found new appetites for knowledge when they spoke to him. To someone who came in asking for the latest novel he might sell not only the novel but a biological treatise on the life of ants, an ecological study of ancient man, a philosophical work, and a history of small sailing-craft.

With maps he was of course remarkable. He had a way of unfolding a map that was nothing less than erotic, a carto-graphical seduction. People bought from him stacks of maps and whole atlases of places to which they would never travel, because Jachin-Boaz had made the coloured images of oceans and continents, roads, cities, rivers and ports irresistible to them.

Jachin-Boaz was gay and tireless at his work, and he looked forward eagerly to each evening with Gretel. At that time they needed very little sleep, made love greedily, talked for hours and took long walks late at night. To Jachin-Boaz the street lamps seemed luminous fruits bursting with knowledge. He tasted their light in his mouth and marvelled that this was he, Jachin-Boaz, tasting the night and the love he had found in the great city. He felt strongly the ripe blackness of rooftops against the night sky, the poignancy of roofs and domes of the city fitting into the night sky. The colours and textures of the pavement, the substance of it, were intense with flavour. His and Gretel's footsteps on the bridges over the river sounded miraculous with truth.

Gretel was nearly twenty years younger than Jachin-Boaz, and he had begun to fall in love with her when he heard her talk about the father she had never known.

Jachin-Boaz's father had been a tall handsome man who had built up his map business from nothing, smoked expensive cigars, directed plays in the local dramatic society, had a beautiful mistress, wanted his son to be a scientist, and died when Jachin-Boaz was still a student.

Jachin-Boaz's wife's father had been a grocer in the town who owned a place in the desert that he wanted to make green with trees and orange groves. For years he impoverished his family by sending money to the desert place. It was not yet green when he took his wife and children there and died. They came back to the town.

Gretel had grown up without a father, had never seen him. He had been killed in the war when she was less than a year old. Her mother had never married again.

Jachin-Boaz had met Gretel when buying books at her shop. He was a regular customer, and in time he invited her to lunch. She was a tall fair blue-eyed girl, full of country freshness. She was as rosy, as sweet and pretty as a lady on a cigar-box lid. They spoke of the places they had come from. Gretel's town was only a few miles away from a famous camp where thousands of Jachin-Boaz's people had died in gas chambers and had risen in smoke from the chimneys of crematoria. Gretel told Jachin-Boaz about her dead father who had been a soldier in the medical corps.

She had only a few things to tell. He had been a market gardener, and her mother and her brother continued in that business. He had drawn a little. There was a charcoal drawing of a heath at home that she had looked at and thought about.

He had played the violin. She had seen music exercise-books of his. She had spoken to a pianist friend of his who remembered playing sonatas with him. He had been an amateur astrologer, and had himself cast the horoscope that foretold his death in the war.

Jachin-Boaz listened to her speak softly about the dead man whom she had not known. He wondered in what features of hers, in what gestures and movements her father survived, in what thoughts and recognitions. He had never known a woman to hold a man so gently in her mind as Gretel held her unknown father. He had never before known a woman with such a gentle mind. She had never known a man with whom she felt so much herself, felt that her essential self mattered so much, was so valued. They fell in love.

The first time they made love Jachin-Boaz was almost beside himself with the achievement of it. This tall fair girl, the daughter of warriors, naked under him, looking up at him in fear and joy, delight and proud submission! He, the son of scholars, bent-backed men in black, generations of studious fugitives. My seed into your womb, he thought. My seed in the warrior-girl's belly. At the same time it was as if he was taking the most hotly desired girl of his boyhood, unapproachable then and a middle-aged woman now, into the bushes of carnal innocence and joy. He was her strong and cunning old man. Jachin-Boaz was enormously pleased with himself.

He was delighted to find that he did not love Gretel for any reason that he might have thought good in the past. Not for intelligence or accomplishments. Not for anything that she did. He loved her simply because she was. What a thing, thought Jachin-Boaz. Love without purpose.

He hired a small van, triumphantly moved her belongings from her room to his flat. She asserted her domestic status by cleaning it. Cautiously she approached the clutter on his desk that Saturday while he was taking a nap. This could be dangerous, she thought, but I have to do it. I can't hold back.

Jachin-Boaz, unsleeping, heard her move every object and all the papers on the desk as she dusted. I don't care, he thought. Even if she throws everything out of the window I love her.

Gretel had examined the master-map in her cleaning. 'I don't think that you made that map for your son,' she said when he told her about it. 'I think you made it for yourself.'

'Do you really think that?' said Jachin-Boaz.

'Yes. And the map brought you to me, so I'm well pleased with it.'

Jachin-Boaz touched the smooth skin of her waist, traced with his finger the curve of her hip. 'It's astonishing,' he said. 'For eighteen years I was alive and you weren't even in the world yet. You were one year old when I got married. You're so young!'

'Make me old,' said Gretel. 'Use me up. Wear me out.'

'I can't make you old,' said Jachin-Boaz. 'But you think you can make me young, eh?'

'I can't make you anything,' said Gretel, 'except maybe comfortable sometimes, I think. But I don't think there ever was a young Jachin-Boaz until the old one took his map and ran away. So now there's a Jachin-Boaz that never was before, and I have him.'

Sometimes, riding in the underground trains, he would see from the corner of his eye the headlines of newspapers being read by other passengers. JACHIN-BOAZ GUILTY, they said. When he looked again the words changed to the usual affairs of the world.

# 6

Boaz-Jachin had completed his first drawing. It was an accurate full-size copy of the dying lion and the two arrows and the two spears that were killing him.

Now by transferring the lines of that drawing to another sheet of brown paper he made a second drawing. It was the same as the first except that one of the arrows was no longer in the lion. It lay on the ground under his hind feet as if it had missed him.

As he looked at the photograph from time to time Boaz-Jachin began to pay more attention to the wheel. He remembered the stillness of the original stone under his eyes and under his fingers when he had touched it. Always and always the leaping dying lion never reaching the splendid blank-faced king for ever receding before him, for ever borne away in safety by the tall wheel for ever turning. It made no difference that the king was now as dead as the lion. The king would always escape.

'The wheel,' said Boaz-Jachin aloud. Because it *was* the wheel, and the wheel was *the* wheel. The sculptor had known it and now it made itself known to Boaz-Jachin as its turning took away his father and his map and brought the dark shop and the bell and the door and the waiting. Boaz-Jachin was sorry that the wheel had made itself known to him. He wished that he had not recognized the wheel.

Boaz-Jachin shook his head. 'Biting the wheel is not enough,' he said.

The door of his room was open, and his mother appeared in the doorway. Her hair was disarranged and she seemed unable to compose her face. There was a knife in her hand. 'Still the school project?' she said.

'Yes,' said Boaz-Jachin. 'What are you doing with the knife?'

'Opening letters,' she said. She paused, then said, 'Don't hate your father. He's sick in his mind, sick in his soul. He's mad. There's something missing in him, there's an emptiness where there should be something.'

'I don't hate him,' said Boaz-Jachin. 'I don't think I feel anything for him.'

'We married too young,' she said. 'My house, the house of my mother and father, seemed to be crouching over me. I wanted to get away. Not to the place in the desert where the money went, not to that place that was a lie, that place that would never be green. They sat in the living room listening to the news on the radio. On Sundays the pattern of the carpet filled me with despair, became a jungle that would swallow me up.' She passed her hand across her eyes. 'We could have made our own green place. I wanted him to be what he could be. I wanted him to be the most and the best that he could be, wanted him to use what was in him. No. Always the turning away, the failure. Always the desert and the dry wind that dries everything up. I'm not ugly even now. Once I was beautiful. The night that I knew I loved him I locked myself in the bathroom and cried. I knew that he would make me unhappy, give me pain. I knew. Your father is a murderer. He killed me. He took away your future. He's mad, but I don't hate him. He doesn't know what he's done. He's lost, lost, lost.' She went out, closing the door behind her. Boaz-Jachin listened to her footsteps going irregularly down the hall, down the stairs to her room.

He finished the second drawing and went down to the shop to get another sheet of brown wrapping-paper. Most of the maps on the walls had been slashed with a knife. Drawers had been pulled out and maps scattered on the floor.

Boaz-Jachin ran up the stairs to his mother's room. The knife lay on the bedside table. Beside it stood an empty sleeping-tablet bottle. His mother was asleep or unconscious. He had no idea how many tablets had been in the bottle.

'Biting the wheel is not enough,' said Boaz-Jachin as he called the doctor.

# 7

Jachin-Boaz dreamed of his father who had died when Jachin-Boaz was in his first year at university. In the dream he was at his father's funeral, but he was younger than university age. He was a little boy, and with his mother he walked up to the coffin among flowers whose fragrance was strong and deathly. His father lay with closed eyes, his face rouged and smoothed-out and blank, his brows unfrowning, his beard pointing out from his chin like a cannon. His hands were crossed on his breast, and the dead left hand held a rolled-up map. The map was rolled with its face outward, and Jachin-Boaz could see a bit of blue ocean, a bit of land, red lines, blue lines, black lines, roads and railways. Lettered neatly on the border were the words *For my son Jachin-Boaz.*

Jachin-Boaz dared not reach for the map, dared not take it from his father's dead hand. He looked at his mother and pointed to the map. She took a pair of scissors from inside her dress, cut off the end of the dead man's beard and showed it to Jachin-Boaz.

'No,' said Jachin-Boaz to his mother who had changed into his wife. 'I want the map. It was in his left hand, not his right. Left for me.'

His wife shook her head. 'You're too little to have one,' she said. It was dark suddenly, and they were in bed. Jachin-Boaz reached out to touch his wife, found the coffin between them and tried to push it away.

The bedside table fell with a crash, and Jachin-Boaz woke up. 'Left, not right,' he said in his own language. 'Left for me.'

'What's the matter?' said Gretel, sitting up in bed. They always spoke English. She could not understand what he was saying.

'It's mine, and I'm big enough to have it,' said Jachin-Boaz, still in his own language. 'What map is it, what ocean, what time is there?'

'Wake up,' said Gretel in English. 'Are you all right?'

'What time are we?' said Jachin-Boaz in English.

'Do you mean what time is it?' said Gretel.

'Where is the time?' said Jachin-Boaz.

'Quarter past five,' said Gretel.

'That's not where it is,' said Jachin-Boaz. His dream had gone out of his mind. He could remember none of it.

# 8

Boaz-Jachin's mother had her stomach pumped, and she stayed in bed for two days. 'I don't know what all the excitement was about,' she said at first. 'There were only two tablets left in the bottle. I wasn't trying to kill myself—I just hadn't been able to sleep, and one tablet never helped.'

'How was I to know?' said Boaz-Jachin. 'All I saw was what you'd done in the shop and then the knife and the empty bottle.'

Later his mother said, 'You saved my life. You and the doctor saved my life.'

'I thought you said there were only two tablets left in the bottle,' said Boaz-Jachin.

His mother tossed her head, looked sideways at him darkly. What a fool you must be, said the look.

But Boaz-Jachin did not know which to believe—the two-tablet story or the dark look. There's no knowing what she might do now, he thought. She might very well turn into some kind of invalid and I'll have to take care of her. The bell jingling at the door and her voice calling from upstairs. He's run away and left me to clean up after him. Boaz-Jachin stayed home from school for the two days that his mother spent in bed, and Lila came to the house in the evening and cooked for them.

Boaz-Jachin made love with Lila in the dark shop at night, on the floor between the map cabinets. In the darkness he looked at the dim gleam of her body, its places that he knew now.

'This is one map he can't take away from me,' he said. They laughed in the dark shop.

Boaz-Jachin made a third drawing: again the dying lion leaping up at the chariot, biting the wheel. But now both arrows were out of him, both arrows were lying on the ground under his feet. The two spears were still at his throat.

He made a fourth drawing: both arrows and one of the spears under the lion's feet.

He made a fifth drawing in which both arrows and both spears lay on the ground under the lion's feet, and he took the evening bus to the town near the ruins of the last king's palace. He carried nothing with him but the rolled-up drawings.

Again he walked from the bus station out to the silent road under the yellow lights. This time the crickets, the distant barking of the dogs, the stones of the roadside under his feet no longer had the sound of being far from everything: they were the sounds of the place where he was.

When he came to the citadel he threw the roll of drawings over the chain-link fence and climbed over it as before. Again the guards were drinking coffee at the fluorescent-lit window. In the moonlight he went to the building where the lion-hunt reliefs were. As before, the door was unlocked.

Boaz-Jachin opened the door, and the lion-hunt hall with the moonlight coming through the skylight was now a place where he had been. It was a place of his time, a home-place. Here he had awakened and come out of a dark cupboard, had wept before the lion-king and the chariot-king. Here he had spoken his name and the name of his father. He knew the place, the place knew him.

Boaz-Jachin walked formally down the middle of the hall in the light of the moon that shone in through the skylights. He stopped in front of the dying lion-king silvered with dim moonlight, leaping up at the chariot that for ever bore the king away.

Boaz-Jachin unrolled his drawings, took stones out of his pocket to hold them flat on the floor.

Boaz-Jachin laid his first drawing on the floor before the lion-king. In his drawing, as in the relief before him, the lion had two arrows in him, two spears at his throat.

'The arrows burn like fire and our strength is fading,' said Boaz-Jachin. 'The spears are sharp and killing. The turning wheel bears us on to darkness.'

He took the second drawing, laid it over the first.

'One of the arrows is drawn,' he said. 'The flesh that bled is whole, unhurt.'

He laid the third drawing over the second.

'The second arrow is drawn,' he said. 'The darkness is fading. Strength is coming back.'

He laid the fourth drawing over the third.

'The first spear lies under our feet. The spearman of the king is empty-handed,' he said.

He laid the fifth drawing over the fourth, then stepped back. In the moonlight the lion-king's eyes looked out at him from the shadow of his brows.

'The second spear, the last weapon, the spear of the king, lies under our feet,' said Boaz-Jachin. 'We rise up on the turning wheel, alive and strong, undying. There is nothing between us and the king.'

# 9

The city was quiet, the birds were singing, and the sky was losing its darkness. The clock said half-past four. Jachin-Boaz could sleep no longer. He got out of bed, dressed, made himself a cup of coffee, and went out.

The street was wet, and on the pavement lay wet blossoms from the trees that overhung the railings. The street gleamed under the blueish light of the street lamps and the blue before-dawn light of the sky. A crow cawed, flapping slowly overhead to settle on a chimney-pot. A taxi hissed softly down the street, passing once, twice, over manhole covers, double-clanging each time. A telephone kiosk, like a large red lantern, lit the drooping blossoms of a chestnut tree.

Jachin-Boaz's footsteps had an early-morning sound. His footsteps, thought Jachin-Boaz, were abroad at all hours. Sometimes he joined them, sometimes not.

Ahead of him were the river and the dark bulk of the bridge under its lamps against the paling sky. Jachin-Boaz heard a manhole cover clang, and found himself waiting for the second clang that would be the sound of the lifted edge dropping back. He had heard no cars passing. There was no second clang.

He looked back over his shoulder and saw, less than a hundred feet away in the blue dawn, a lion. He was large, massive, with a heavy black mane. He had lifted his head as Jachin-Boaz turned, and now he stood motionless with one paw on the manhole cover. His eyes, catching the light of the street lamps, burned like steady pale green fires under the shadow of his brows.

44

A church clock struck five, and Jachin-Boaz realized that he had heard the lion before he saw him. The hairs on the back of his neck lifted, he felt deathly cold. He had *heard* the lion first. There was no hope that this was like the newspaper headlines, the mind playing a trick on the eyes.

A taxi entered the street, approaching the lion from behind. The lion grunted and turned, the taxi made a U-turn, went back the way it had come. Jachin-Boaz did not move.

The lion turned towards him again, his head thrust forward, his eyes fixed on Jachin-Boaz. He seemed not to move, but only shifted his weight slightly and was closer than before. Again, and closer.

Jachin-Boaz took one step back. The lion stopped, one paw slightly lifted, his eyes always on Jachin-Boaz. The thing is not to run, thought Jachin-Boaz. The lion seemed to be gathering himself. Surely he's too far away to spring, thought Jachin-Boaz. He took another step backwards, trying to move as subtly as the lion had done. This time he saw the rise and fall of the lion's shoulders, the sliding of his heavy paws.

Jachin-Boaz, backing towards the bridge, had reached the corner, his eyes still fixed on the lion. To the right and left behind him lay the road along the embankment. He heard a taxi coming over the bridge, turned his head just enough to see that the FOR HIRE sign was lit. He raised his arm to signal, pointing along the embankment.

The taxi turned right as it came off the bridge and pulled up beside Jachin-Boaz. He was still facing the lion, with his back to the taxi.

The driver slid the window down. 'Do you want to go backwards or forwards?' he said.

Jachin-Boaz felt for the door handle behind him, opened

the door, got in. He gave the driver the address of the book-shop where he worked.

The taxi pulled away. Through the rear window Jachin-Boaz saw the lion standing motionless, head lifted.

The taxi hummed along smoothly. There was full day-light now, and there were other cars ahead, behind, on both sides. Jachin-Boaz leaned back. Then he leaned for-ward, lowered the panel in the glass partition between him and the driver.

'Did you see anything back there where you picked me up?' he said.

The driver looked up at Jachin-Boaz's face in the rear-view mirror and nodded his head. 'Proper big one, weren't it?'

Jachin-Boaz felt giddy. 'Then why didn't you ... Why didn't you ... ' He didn't know what he wanted the driver to have done.

The driver looked straight ahead as the taxi hummed through the traffic. 'It's nothing to me,' he said. 'I thought it was yours.'

# IO

After offering his drawings before the lion-king Boaz-Jachin burned them on the plain where the lions had been killed. He took a large metal trash basket from the refreshment stand, put his drawings in it and set them afire.

He expected the guards to see the flames, and stood near the spectator's hill where he would have a chance of dodging out of sight when they came. No one came. The flames leaped up, sparks and flakes of charred paper drifted over the plain, the fire died quickly.

Boaz-Jachin climbed over the chain-link fence again, walked back to the town, and slept in the bus station.

He felt cosy in the bus going home. He felt cool and easy, clean and empty, as he did after making love with Lila. He thought of the road to the citadel of the dead king, how he had felt walking on it each time. Like the lion-hunt hall, it was his place now, printed on the map of his mind. Its daylight and its darkness were in him now, its crickets and its barking dogs and stones. He could travel that road when he liked, wherever he might be.

When Boaz-Jachin got home his mother was out. He was glad to be alone, glad not to have to speak. He went to his room and took out his unfinished map. He put Lila's house on it, the last king's palace, the plain where the lions had been killed, the hill he had sat on, the road he had walked, and the two bus stations.

His mother came home and made dinner. At the table she spoke of the difficulties of managing the shop, of her constant tiredness, of how little she was able to sleep and how much weight she had lost. Sometimes Boaz-Jachin saw her face waiting for a reply but he could not always remember what she had been saying. Her face became strange to him, and he became strange to himself. Again he felt empty, but it was not the easy emptiness that he had had in the bus. It was as if something had gone out of him and now he must follow it into the world. He was restless, and wanted to be moving on.

'Why?' said his mother.

'Why what?' said Boaz-Jachin.

'Why are you looking at me that way, I said,' said his mother. 'What are you thinking about? You look a thousand miles away from here.'

'I don't know,' said Boaz-Jachin. 'I don't think I was thinking about anything.' He was thinking, maybe I'll never see you again.

Late that night he went down to the shop and looked at one of the big wall-maps. He looked at his country on it and the place where his town was. He ran his finger over the smooth surface, felt the lines of seeking that led from his town and other towns, his country and other countries, converging on a great city far away across the sea. His father, he thought, would be there, and with him would be the master-map he had promised to Boaz-Jachin.

He went to the office, opened the cash box. It was empty. His mother, then, had noticed the absence and return of the money that he had taken the other time. Boaz-Jachin shrugged. He had enough money of his own to live on for two weeks or so if he slept rough, and he had his guitar.

He packed his rucksack, put his map in it, took his guitar. He left a note for his mother:

I am going to find my father and get my map.

He went to Lila's house and slipped a note under the door:

> I thought that I would ask you to come with me
> but I have to go alone.

Boaz-Jachin walked out through the sleeping town, past the palm trees and the square where the jet of the fountain continually rose and fell, past dark shops and houses and dogs that went their several ways, past bright closed petrol stations. He walked out to the road, heard the stones of the roadside rolling under his feet, felt the night in the road and the morning that was coming.

# II

The taxi driver had winked when Jachin-Boaz paid him. So he didn't see the lion, thought Jachin-Boaz. He saw that I was a foreigner and thought that I was drunk, and he was making fun of me.

The lion was not at the bookshop when Jachin-Boaz got out of the taxi, nor was there any sign of him that day. Jachin-Boaz had been in mortal terror when the lion was stalking him, but there was a strange joy in him afterwards. Lions were extinct. There were no lions any more. But he had a lion. 'I thought it was yours,' the taxi driver had said, having his joke with the foreigner he thought was drunk.

He *is* mine, thought Jachin-Boaz. There is a lion, and that lion, real or unreal, has the power to accomplish my death. I know it. But he's my lion and I'm glad that he exists, even though I'm in terror of him.

Jachin-Boaz went to a nearby coffee shop and walked back and forth in front of it like a sentry until it opened. Thinking about the lion he felt himself walking differently, set apart from other men, marked out for a danger, possibly a death, that was unique. He carried himself with melancholy pride, like an exiled king.

When the café opened he sat drinking coffee and looking out at the people who passed. He felt new and sharply defined, newly found by himself and fatefully alone among millions, as if he had just stepped from an aeroplane. Everything that is found is lost again, he thought for the first time. And yet nothing that is found is lost again.

What is a map? There is only one place, and that place is time. I am in the time where a lion has been found.

All day in the bookshop the lion lived in his mind. He had no doubt that the lion would appear again and he wondered how he, Jachin-Boaz, would comport himself at the next encounter. He did not know whether the lion was real in the sense that he himself and the shop and the street were real. But he knew that the lion could kill him.

At home that evening he was very gay, and made love with Gretel suavely and greedily, feeling like an international traveller, a man of wealth, a connoisseur of wines. He went to sleep with the figure of the lion in his mind as he had seen him last — head uplifted in the first light of day, stern and demanding, like a patriotic duty silently calling.

Again he woke up at half-past four. Gretel was sleeping soundly. Jachin-Boaz bathed, shaved, and dressed. From the back of the shelves under the larder where he had hidden it he took a paper-wrapped package, put it into a carrier bag. Then he went out.

He walked down the street to the road along the embankment, stopped at the corner and looked back. He saw nothing.

Jachin-Boaz crossed to the river side of the road and walked beside the parapet looking at the river and the boats rocking at their moorings. He passed the next bridge, and the sky through its webwork was brightening.

It was this bright when I looked back at him through the taxi window, thought Jachin-Boaz. I wonder if he stops being there when it's broad daylight.

The sky over the river was massed with dark clouds and dramatic lights, like skies in marine paintings. The river ran lapping and gurgling by the wall. The road along the embankment awoke to cars in twos and threes, a cyclist, a running man in a tracksuit, a young couple walking, holding last night's darkness between their close-together faces, their long hair mingled.

Jachin-Boaz was tired, he had had too little sleep, his expectation seemed foolish now. He turned and walked back the way he had come.

The young couple who had passed him were sitting on a bench, embracing sleepily. On the pavement beside them sat the lion, looking at Jachin-Boaz.

Jachin-Boaz had been looking at the river, and was no more than five yards from the lion when he saw him. The lion's head came forward. He crouched, lashing his tail. His eyes were mystical, luminous, infinite. Jachin-Boaz smelled the lion. Hot sun, dry wind and the tawny plains.

Jachin-Boaz dared not move a single step. Never taking his eyes from the lion he reached into the carrier bag for the package that was there, let the bag fall so that both hands would be free. With shaking hands he unwrapped the five pounds of beefsteak he had brought with him. He threw it to the lion, almost falling as he did it. The meat landed with a wet and solid smack.

The lion, still crouching, came forward and ate the meat, growling and staring at Jachin-Boaz. When Jachin-Boaz saw the lion eating the meat all courage left him. He would have fainted if the lion had not moved.

The lion finished the meat and sprang at Jachin-Boaz. Jachin-Boaz, with a scream, flung himself over the parapet and into the river.

He came to the surface choking and retching from the filthy water he had swallowed, and looked up as the current carried him swiftly on. He saw the two pale faces of the young couple above the top of the parapet, bobbing up and down and moving along with him. No lion.

Jachin-Boaz swam close to the wall, letting the current

carry him along to the concrete steps that came down to the water. There he dragged himself ashore, staggered up the steps, and stopped at the locked gate that shut the steps off from the pavement. He looked in all directions but did not see the lion.

The young man and the girl were standing before him, faces pale, wild hair wilder than before. They reached forward to help him over the gate but Jachin-Boaz, still trembling violently, was able to climb over it by himself.

'You all right?' said the young man. 'What happened?'

'Yes, I'm all right, thank you,' said Jachin-Boaz in his own language. 'What did you see?'

The young man and the girl shook their heads apologetically, and Jachin-Boaz said again, in English, 'Thank you. What did you see?'

'We saw you stop near us, unwrap some meat, and throw it on the pavement,' said the girl.

'Then the meat jerked and jumped about,' said the young man, 'and it tore itself up and disappeared. Then you screamed and jumped into the river. What happened?'

'That's all you saw?' said Jachin-Boaz.

'That's all,' said the young man. 'Are you sure you're all right? Don't you need help? What happened to the meat? How did you make it do that? Why did you jump into the river?'

'Are you a hypnotist?' said the girl.

Jachin-Boaz, foul-smelling from the river and standing in a spreading puddle, shook his head.

'It's all right,' he said. 'I don't know. Thank you very much.' He turned and walked home slowly and weakly, stopping often to look behind him.

# 12

Boaz-Jachin stood at the roadside. His rucksack was on his back. His black guitar-case, hot from the sun, stood leaning against him. The road shimmered in the heat. He was no more than fifty miles from home, and he wondered if his mother had sent the police after him. Cars whined past like bullets, followed by long stretches of emptiness and silence.

An old humpbacked-looking open lorry loaded with oranges came puttering up and stopped with a mingled reek of petrol, oranges, and orange-crate wood. The driver leaned out of the window. He wore an old black felt hat from which the brim had been cut. What remained was too big for a skullcap and too small for a fez. His face had too much expression.

'Where are you going?' said the driver.

'To the seaport,' said Boaz-Jachin.

'Get in,' said the driver.

Boaz-Jachin got in and put his rucksack and guitar on the shelf behind the seat.

'What's in the guitar-case?' said the driver, raising his voice above the roar and rattle of the lorry as they pulled away.

'A guitar,' said Boaz-Jachin.

'It doesn't hurt to ask,' said the driver. 'It could be a machine-gun. You can't tell me that everybody with a guitar-case is carrying a guitar. The laws of probability are against it.'

'In the films I think the gangsters use violin cases,' said Boaz-Jachin.

'That's in the films,' said the driver. 'Real life is something else. Real life is full of surprises.'

'Yes,' said Boaz-Jachin, yawning. He leaned his head against the back of the seat and closed his eyes, smelling the petrol, the oranges, and the orange-crate wood.

'Films,' said the driver. 'Always the films are full of men with guns. Why do you think that is?'

'I don't know,' said Boaz-Jachin. 'People like excitement, violence.'

'Always in the film posters,' said the driver, 'the hero is pointing with a gun, shooting with a gun. Because we men feel ourselves to be gunless. You follow me?'

'No,' said Boaz-Jachin.

'I've talked to professional men – scholars, lecturers,' said the driver. 'It's a widespread emotional condition. We men feel ourselves to be weaponless. You know what I mean?'

'No,' said Boaz-Jachin.

The driver put his hand between Boaz-Jachin's legs, gripped him firmly, took his hand away before Boaz-Jachin could react.

'That's what I mean,' said the driver. 'A man's weapon.'

Boaz-Jachin took his rucksack from the shelf behind the seat and put it in his lap.

'Why'd you do that?' said the driver.

Boaz-Jachin said nothing.

The driver nodded his head bitterly, looking at the road, both hands on the steering-wheel.

'They should rather make films about the women who take away our guns,' he said. 'Nobody wants the truth.'

'You can drop me off in this town we're coming to,' said Boaz-Jachin. 'I have an uncle here that I have to see before I go to the port.'

'I don't believe you,' said the driver. 'You didn't say anything about your uncle when I picked you up.'

'I forgot,' said Boaz-Jachin. 'But I have to see him. I have to get out here.'

They were almost at the edge of the town. The lorry, roaring and rattling, did not slow down.

'I can stick my head out of the window and yell for help,' said Boaz-Jachin.

'Go ahead,' said the driver. 'You look like a runaway to me. If you make trouble I can always turn you over to the police.'

The town flew by on either side: chickens, dogs, children, houses, petrol pumps, awnings, shops, vans, cars, lorries, soft-drink machines, a barber pole, a cinema, petrol pumps, houses, children, dogs, chickens. The lorry roared and rattled. The town grew small in the rear-view mirror.

'You are cruel,' said the driver. 'You are cruel like all the young. You come out into the world, you want this and that. "Take me here, take me there," you say to the world. You don't look at the people who offer friendship along with the ride or the food or whatever you hold out your hand for. You don't see their faces. For them you have no feelings.'

'If I'd known you were going to get so worked up over giving me a ride I wouldn't have taken it,' said Boaz-Jachin.

'You're going to the seaport,' said the driver. 'What will you do there?'

'Work my passage on a boat if I can,' said Boaz-Jachin, 'or earn money so I can pay for it.'

'Doing what?' said the driver.

'I don't know. Playing the guitar. Waiting on tables. Working on the docks. Whatever I can do.'

'Where are you going with the boat?'

'Why do you have to know everything?'

'Why shouldn't I know everything I can find out? Is it a big secret where you're going with the boat?'

'To look for my father,' said Boaz-Jachin.

'Ah-h-h!' said the driver, as if he had finally worked a bit of meat out of the tooth it was stuck in. 'To look for the father! The father ran away?'

'Yes.'

'Your mother has a new man and you don't like him?'

Boaz-Jachin tried to imagine his mother with someone other than his father. His mind gave him pictures of the two of them together. When he took his father out of the pictures he had nothing else to put there. Would his father have a new woman? He took the mother out of the mind-pictures. The father simply looked alone, subtracted from. He shook his head. 'My mother hasn't got anyone,' he said.

'What do you want from your father, that you're looking for him?'

Boaz-Jachin thought the word *map*, and it became a no-word, a word that he had never seen or heard, a sound without meaning. Something very big, something very small, seemed present in his mind, but in his mind there seemed no place for him. He squirmed in his seat. The lorry driver in his strange hat with his face that had too much expression suddenly seemed a no-person. Lion, thought Boaz-Jachin, but felt only the emptiness where something had gone out of him. He saw the map of Lila's body spread on the floor in the dark shop. Gone. No map.

'Well?' said the driver.

'He promised me something,' said Boaz-Jachin.

'Money, property, an education?'

'Something else,' said Boaz-Jachin. 'I don't want to talk about it.'

'Something else,' said the driver. 'Something private, noble, sacred even, such as can only be between men. And what will you bring him?'

'Nothing,' said Boaz-Jachin. 'There's nothing he wants from me.'

'You're a real giver,' said the driver. He sighed heavily. 'Parents are a mystery. Sometimes I think about my father and mother for ten or fifteen miles at a stretch. My father was a prosperous and well-known man, an intellectual. Every morning he read the newspaper from front to back, straight through, and said many profound things. My mother was a whore.'

'What was your father?' said Boaz-Jachin.

'A pimp,' said the driver, 'and a homosexual as well. Classical profession, classical principles. Sometimes he made love with my mother as a special favour, but he never intended to have children. I represent the triumph of whoring over pimping.

'My mother always said that fatherhood broke my father's spirit. He left us when I was five. I grew up among black silk underwear, pink kimonos, the smell of last night's drinks in smeary glasses, ash trays full of dead cigarettes, and antiseptic.

'Be your own father and your own son is what I always say. That way you can have many long talks with yourself, and if you're often disappointed you're no worse off than every other father and son. Black silk underwear is very smooth against the skin when you're alone.'

Underwhere, thought Boaz-Jachin. Under our where we wear our underwhere. I have no underwhere. The road to the citadel, the roadside stones, the hill, the lion-coloured plain, the tawny motion, the lion-king, the emptiness where he has gone from. I have underwhere, thought Boaz-Jachin. 'I think my father was disappointed in me,' he said.

'More likely in himself,' said the driver. 'You should make love with strangers whenever you can.'

'What's that got to do with my father?' said Boaz-Jachin.

'Nothing. Your father isn't the only thing in the world.'

'Why with strangers?' said Boaz-Jachin.

'Because that's the only kind of person there is,' said the driver. 'When you get to know a face or a voice or a smell you think the person isn't a stranger, but that's a lie. With an unknown face and the nakedness of an unknown body the whole thing is purer.'

Boaz-Jachin was silent listening to the noise of the lorry and smelling the petrol, the oranges, the orange-crate wood.

'I go back and forth on this road all the time,' said the driver. 'Always there are new unknown faces on it, new faces coming out into the world, heading for the port. I go to the port, come back again always.'

Boaz-Jachin hugged his rucksack to himself in silence.

The lorry slowed down, the roar separated into individual putterings, rattles, and squeaks. The driver pulled into a layby, stopped the lorry, shut off the motor. He put his hand on Boaz-Jachin's knee.

'Don't,' said Boaz-Jachin.

'Just for a little while,' begged the driver. 'On the road between the past and the future. Just for a little while give me your strangerhood, your strangeness and your newness. Give me some of you. Be my father, my son, my brother, my friend. Be something to me for a little while.'

'No,' said Boaz-Jachin. 'I can't. I'm sorry.'

The driver began to cry. 'I'm sorry I bothered you,' he said. 'Please leave me now. I need to be alone. Go away, please.' He reached past Boaz-Jachin and opened the door.

Boaz-Jachin took his guitar from the shelf behind the seat and got out. The door slammed shut.

Boaz-Jachin wanted to give the lorry driver something. He opened his rucksack, looked for something that could be a gift. 'Wait!' he called above the roar of the engine as the lorry started up again.

But the driver had not heard him. Boaz-Jachin saw his

face still crying under the old black brimless hat that was not a skullcap and not a fez as the lorry, trailing its aroma of petrol, oranges, and orange-crate wood, pulled out into the road and away.

Boaz-Jachin closed the rucksack, buckled the flap. There was nothing in it that could have been a gift for the lorry driver.

# 13

Jachin-Boaz continued to wake up very early in the mornings, always with the knowledge that the lion was waiting
somewhere in the streets for him. But since he had seen him
eat real meat he dared not go out until the rest of the world
was awake and moving about. He did not see the lion
during business hours or in the evening. He was in a state
of excitement most of the time.

'You make love as if you're saying hello for the first
time and goodbye for the last,' Gretel told him. 'Will you
be here tomorrow?'

'If there's a tomorrow for me I'll be here if here is where
I am,' said Jachin-Boaz.

'Who could ask for more?' said Gretel. 'You're a reliable
man. You're a rock.'

Jachin-Boaz thought about the lion constantly—how
he had eaten real meat, how the young couple had not seen
the lion but had seen the meat being eaten. He dared not
encounter the lion again without some kind of professional
advice.

He spoke guardedly to the owner of the bookshop.
'Modern life,' said Jachin-Boaz, 'particularly modern life
in cities, creates great tensions in people, don't you think?'

'Modern life, ancient life,' said the owner. 'Where there's
life there's tension.'

'Yes,' said Jachin-Boaz. 'Tension and nerves. It's astonishing, really, what nerves can do.'

'Well, they have a system, you see,' said the owner.
'When you suffer an attack of nerves you're being attacked

by the nervous system. What chance has a man got against a system?'

'Exactly,' said Jachin-Boaz. 'He could have delusions, hallucinations.'

'Happens every day of the week,' said the owner. 'Sometimes I, for example, have the delusion that this shop is a business. Then I come back to reality and realize that it's just an expensive hobby.'

'But people who have hallucinations,' Jachin-Boaz persisted, 'powerful hallucinations — what's to be done for them?'

'What kind of powerful hallucinations do you have in mind?' said the owner.

'Well, say a carnivorous one,' said Jachin-Boaz. 'Just for the sake of argument.'

'A carnivorous hallucination,' said the owner. 'Could you give me an example of such a thing?'

'Yes,' said Jachin-Boaz. 'Suppose a man saw a dog, let's say, that wasn't really there in the usual way, so to speak. Nobody else but the man can see the dog. The man feeds the dog dog food, and everyone sees the dog food eaten by the dog they can't see.'

'Quite an unusual hallucination,' said the owner, 'to say nothing of the expense of keeping it. What breed of hallucinatory dog is it?'

'Well, I'm not actually thinking of a dog,' said Jachin-Boaz. 'I was speaking hypothetically, just to give an idea of the sort of thing that's on my mind — the way reality and illusion can sometimes get mixed up and all that. Nothing to do with dogs. What I had in mind was perhaps to consult a professional man about it. Can you recommend someone?'

'I have a friend who's a psychiatrist,' said the owner, 'if you're talking about something that has to do with the mind. On the other hand, if it eats real dog food, I don't know. And he's expensive.'

'Actually it's nothing terribly pressing,' said Jachin-Boaz. 'I might ring him up or I might not. Sometimes it's good to clear up a thing like that rather than have it on your mind.'

'Certainly,' said the owner. 'If you'd like the afternoon off, you know … '

'Not at all,' said Jachin-Boaz. 'I'm perfectly all right, really.' He rang up the psychiatrist and made an appointment for the next day.

The doctor's office was in a block of flats, on the top floor of four floors of cooking smells. Jachin-Boaz climbed the stairs, rang, let himself in, and sat on a studio couch in a big kitchen until the doctor appeared.

The doctor was short, had long red hair and a beard, and was dressed like a man doing odd jobs around the house on a weekend. He turned on an electric kettle, made tea in a little Chinese teapot, put two little Chinese cups on a tray with the pot, and said, 'Come in.'

They went into the room that was his office and sat on facing chairs. There was a studio couch along one wall. By another stood a big table piled with books and papers, a typewriter, two tape recorders, a briefcase, and several huddles of large brown envelopes and file folders. There were more books and papers on smaller tables, on chairs, on the floor, on the mantelpiece, and on shelves.

'Start wherever you like,' said the doctor.

'I'll start with the lion,' said Jachin-Boaz. 'I can't afford to come more than once, so I'll get to the point immediately.' He told the doctor about his two encounters with the lion, particularly stressing the five pounds of beefsteak.

'And always I know that just before dawn he will be waiting for me somewhere in the streets,' said Jachin-Boaz. 'And of course I know that lions are extinct. There are no lions any more. So he can't be real. *Can* he be real?'

'He eats real meat,' said the doctor. 'You saw him do it, other people saw him do it.'

'That's right,' said Jachin-Boaz. 'And I'm meat.'

'Right,' said the doctor. 'So let's not split hairs about whether he's real. He can do real damage. He's a real problem that has to be coped with one way or another.'

'How?' said Jachin-Boaz, looking at his watch. He was paying for fifty minutes of the doctor's time, and ten of them were gone.

'Try to remember the night before you saw the lion for the first time,' said the doctor. 'Is there anything at all that comes to mind? Any dreams?'

'Nothing,' said Jachin-Boaz.

'The day before the night before?'

'Nothing.'

'Anything happen at work? You said on the telephone that you work at the bookshop.'

'Nothing happened at the bookshop. There was a lion door-stop at the other shop, my own shop where I sold maps before I came to this country.'

'What about the lion door-stop? Anything come to mind?'

'My son said that my map wouldn't show where to find a lion.'

'What about your son?'

'Boaz-Jachin,' said Jachin-Boaz. 'That was my father's name too. He started the business, the map shop. He ran away from his father. I ran away from my son. From my wife and son. My father said that the world was made for seeking and finding. By means of maps everything that is found is never lost again. That's what my father said. But everything that is found is always lost again.'

'What have you lost?'

'Years of myself, my manhood,' said Jachin-Boaz. 'There

64

is only one place, and that place is time. Why do I keep the map that I promised him? I don't need it. I could have left it for him. I could send it to him.'

'To your father?'

'My father's dead. To my son.'

'Why didn't you give it to him?'

'I kept it for myself, kept it for finding what I'd never found.'

'What was that?'

'I want to talk about the lion,' said Jachin-Boaz looking at his watch.

The doctor lit a pipe, using up almost a minute, it seemed to Jachin-Boaz.

'All right,' said the doctor from behind a big cloud of smoke. 'What's the lion? The lion is something that can kill you. What's death?'

'Have we got time to go into that?' said Jachin-Boaz.

'What I mean is, what's death in this context? Is it something you want or something you don't want?'

'Who wants to die?' said Jachin-Boaz.

'You'd be surprised,' said the doctor. 'Let's try to find out what being killed by the lion would be for you.'

'The end,' said Jachin-Boaz.

'Would it be, say, a reward for you?'

'Absolutely not.'

'Would it be, well, what's the opposite of reward?'

'Punishment?' said Jachin-Boaz. 'Yes, I suppose so.'

'For what?'

'My wife and son could tell you that at great length,' said Jachin-Boaz looking at his watch again. 'And meanwhile the lion is waiting out there every morning before dawn.'

'Does he come into the flat or follow you to work?' said the doctor.

'No. But he's *there*, and I know he's there.'

'Right,' said the doctor. 'But the choice is yours whether you meet him or not, yes?'

'Yes.'

'So what we're talking about is that you're afraid you'll go out to meet the meat-eating lion. You're afraid you'll accept the punishment.'

'I hadn't thought of that,' said Jachin-Boaz.

'What kind of people get punished?' said the doctor.

'All kinds, I suppose.'

'The jury goes out to deliberate,' said the doctor. 'The jury comes back in. The judge says, "How do you find the defendant?"'

'Guilty,' said Jachin-Boaz. 'But where does the lion come from? Explain that.'

'All right,' said the doctor. 'I'll go as far as I can with it. But you have to remember that not only don't I have all the answers but I don't even have most of the questions where you're concerned. Let's forget the technicalities. The lion is something extraordinary, but whether he eats meat or plays the clarinet is academic.'

'He wouldn't kill me with a clarinet,' said Jachin-Boaz.

'The lion', continued the doctor, 'is capable of a real effect on you. But that's not much stranger than television, for instance. Right now coming through the air are pictures of people talking, singing, dancing, maybe even pictures of lions. With a television receiver in this room we could see those images. We could hear voices, music, sound effects. We could in reality be emotionally affected by them even though the images would only be images.'

'That's not quite parallel to my lion,' said Jachin-Boaz. 'Also, everybody with a television receiver can see the programmes you're talking about. But nobody but me can see my lion.'

'Suppose,' said the doctor, 'that you were the only person

in the world who had a receiver that could pick up this particular broadcast.' He looked at his watch. 'A guilt and punishment receiver.'

Jachin-Boaz looked at his watch. Less than a minute remained. 'But where's the lion coming from?' he said. 'Where's the transmitter?'

'From whom are you expecting punishment?'

'Everybody,' Jachin-Boaz was surprised to hear himself say as his mother and father unexpectedly rose up in his mind. Love us. Be how we want you to be.

'That's as far as we can get now,' said the doctor, standing up. 'We'll have to stop there.'

'But how can I turn off the programme?' said Jachin-Boaz.

'Do you want to?' said the doctor, opening the door.

'What a question!' said Jachin-Boaz. 'Do I want to!' But as the door closed behind him he was adding up the cost of daily beefsteak for the lion.

# 14

Boaz-Jachin sat down in the layby and marked on his map the place where the lorry driver had left him.

He was still sitting there thinking about the lorry driver when a little red convertible with its top down pulled up, playing music. The number plates were foreign and the driver was a deeply tanned handsome woman of about the same age as his mother.

The woman smiled with very white teeth and opened the door. Boaz-Jachin got in. 'Where are you going?' she said in English.

'To the seaport,' said Boaz-Jachin speaking English carefully. 'Where are you going?'

'Different places,' she said. 'I'll take you to the port.' She swung the little red car smoothly out into the road.

Boaz-Jachin, since his encounter with the lorry driver, felt as if his former peaceful state of not knowing anything about people had been peeled from him like the rind from an orange. He doubted that it could be put back. As he sat beside the blonde woman it seemed to him that people's stories were all written on their faces for anyone to read. Perhaps, he thought, he might now be able to converse also with animals, trees, stones. The lion came back to him briefly, like a memory from earliest childhood, then was gone. He felt guilty because he had made the lorry driver cry.

He looked at the blonde woman. She seemed to carry her womanhood the way men on the docks carried baling hooks on one shoulder – shiny, pointed, sharp.

The wind rushed by, blowing their hair. The music was being played by a tape machine. When one side was finished the woman turned over the cassette and there was new music. The music was smooth and full, and it sounded like the marvellous cocktail bars in films where unattainable-looking women and suave violent men understood each other immediately by a look.

Boaz-Jachin knew the blonde woman's story as if she had told him everything. She had been married several times, and was now a wealthy divorcée. She, like the lorry driver, was looking for new faces coming out into the world. She too would want him to be something to her for a little while on the road between the past and the future.

There would be a hotel or a motel on the road, the little red car would pull up and stop, and she would look at him as the film stars looked, with her delicate eyebrows raised, without a word.

The room would be cool and dark, with slitted sunlight coming through the blinds. Ice would tinkle in glasses. She would speak low and huskily, with her lips against his ear. There would be room service, hushed, respectful, and envious—some young man a year or two older than he.

She would be artful and tigerish, would please him in ways unknown to him before, and he would give to her because it was unfair always to take without giving. He would be her stranger, and she his. He would appease the hungry ghost of the lorry driver by his generosity to this woman. It would cost him a few days—she would not want to part with him quickly—but they would both be enriched by it.

Boaz-Jachin thought of the parts of her body that might not be tanned by the sun, how the scent of her flesh would be and the taste of her. He was getting an erection, and crossed his legs discreetly.

Afterwards she would offer him money. He would not accept it of course, although he needed money very badly. On the other hand, he asked himself, was there any difference morally between that and taking money for playing the guitar and singing?

The wind lessened, the music was louder, the car stopped. Boaz-Jachin looked all around for a hotel or motel but saw none. There was a road going off to the right.

'I just remembered,' said the woman, 'I have to turn off here. I'd better drop you now.'

Boaz-Jachin picked up his guitar and his rucksack and got out. The woman closed the door, locked it.

'When a boy your age looks at me the way I think you were looking at me,' she said, 'then one of us is in bad shape. Either I shouldn't think that way or you shouldn't look that way.'

The little red car pulled away, playing music, going straight ahead towards the seaport.

# 15

The analogy of the television broadcast stayed in Jachin-Boaz's mind. He was receiving a lion. The lion was a punishment. His wife and son would of course wish to punish him. Did he want to be punished? Was the lion simply a punishment? He could not arrive at a simple yes or no to either of those questions.

The lion ate real meat. What had it eaten since the five pounds of beefsteak three days ago? Would it be thin now, hungry, its ribs sticking out? If it was a lion that appeared exclusively to him, surely he was responsible for feeding it?

A customer came into the shop and asked for a book on ancient Near-Eastern art. Jachin-Boaz showed him the two paperbacks and the one hardback that were on the shelves and went back to unwrapping the shipment that had come in that morning.

The customer was one of the shop's regulars, and inclined to be chatty over his purchases. 'The lions are quite remarkable,' he said.

Jachin-Boaz stood up from the books, the brown paper and the string, bolt upright and alert.

'What lions?' he said.

'Here,' said the customer, 'in the reliefs in the north palace.' He laid the open book on the counter in front of Jachin-Boaz. 'I suppose the sculptor was bound by convention in his handling of the king and the other human figures, but the lions have immense distinction — each one's an individual tragic portrait. Have you seen the originals?'

'No,' said Jachin-Boaz, 'although I used to live not very far from the ruins.'

'That's how it is,' said the customer. 'Here's one of the artistic wonders of the world, absolutely the high point of the art of its period, and when you live next door to it you don't bother to look at it.'

'Yes,' said Jachin-Boaz, no longer paying attention to the man's words. He was turning the pages, looking at the photographs of the lion-hunt reliefs. He came to the dying lion biting the chariot wheel.

'Easy enough to see where the sculptor's sympathies lay,' said the customer. 'His commission may have been from the king but his heart was with the lion. The king, for all the detail and all the curls in his beard, is little more than an ideograph, a symbol referring to the splendour of kings. But the lion!'

Jachin-Boaz stared fixedly at the lion. He recognized him.

'The king is almost secondary,' said the customer. 'The mortal stretch of the lion's body meets the length of the spears he hurls himself upon, becomes one long diagonal thrust of forces eternally opposed. That thrust is balanced on the turning wheel and the lion's frowning dying face is at the centre, biting the wheel. Masterfully composed, the whole thing. The king *is* secondary, really—a dynamic counterweight. He's only there to hold the spear, and nothing less than a king would be of suitable rank for the death of that lion.'

Yes, thought Jachin-Boaz, there was no mistaking that frown. That was his frown, and the mane grew from the forehead in the same way. The set of shadowy eyes was the same. He had been thinner when he had seen him last, he thought, than he appeared here. And he had given him nothing to eat for days! Was the lion only able to eat food that came from him, Jachin-Boaz? No one else saw him. Did he see anyone else?

Jachin-Boaz seemed with his eyes to be possessing the lion

in the picture beyond the possibility of its belonging to anyone else. The customer felt that his cultivated appreciation was being made unimportant. He began to feel protective towards the book he was buying, and made little patting motions on the counter with his hands. 'I'll have the book,' he said, and took out his chequebook.

'But it's the wheel,' said Jachin-Boaz, his eyes fixed on the implacable eight-spoked studded chariot wheel in the photograph, part of it lost in erosion and the weathering of the stone. 'It's the wheel. He should understand that. It isn't the king. Maybe the king doesn't even want the lion to die. He knows that the lion too is a king, perhaps one greater than himself. It's the wheel, the wheel. That's the whole thing. The sculptor knew it was the wheel and not the king. Biting it doesn't help, but one has to. That's all there is.'

'That's one way of looking at it, of course,' said the customer. 'Really,' he said, looking at his watch, 'I must be moving on.'

'Yes,' said Jachin-Boaz. Mechanically he rang up the sale and wrapped the book, wondering how many pounds of meat were required to keep a lion in good flesh. And of course there must be something cheaper than beefsteak. Horsemeat? Perhaps if he called the zoo they would be able to advise him—he could say tiger instead of lion. Was it possible that the lion didn't know that it was the wheel? But he must know—there was such knowledge in his face.

'Please,' said the customer, 'may I have the book?'

'Yes,' said Jachin-Boaz, putting it at last into the customer's hands and thinking how strange it was that anyone else should carry a photograph of the animal so intimately and oddly connected with him.

He was nervous and jumpy for the rest of the day, putting books in wrong places and forgetting where he'd put them.

73

He moved quickly and suddenly from one part of the shop to another without remembering why he went where he did. His mind darted from one thought to another.

He dreaded the lion, trembled and went cold at the thought of him, but at the same time craved the sight of him. The feeding of the lion now seemed his responsibility, his peculiar obligation, and he worried about the expense of it.

Jachin-Boaz rang up the zoo, said that he was doing research for a magazine article, and asked how much meat a full-grown tiger would require daily. He waited while the young lady at the zoo made inquiries. When she returned to the telephone he was told that the tigers each received a twelve-pound joint six days a week and were starved for one day.

'Twelve pounds,' said Jachin-Boaz.

Well, actually that included the bones, she said. The meat in such a joint might be six or seven pounds.

How long could a lion ... tiger, he meant to say, go without food?

Another absence from the phone. Five to seven days, she said on her return. Tigers in a wild state might consume forty to sixty pounds at one time, then go hungry for a week. Certainly one could say that they were able to go without eating for five to seven days.

Where did they buy the meat for the tigers?

They bought condemned meat, he was told, and was given the name of the butchers who sold it.

Condemned meat! thought Jachin-Boaz after he had rung off. The thought made him uncomfortable. Condemned meat, no. He would economize somewhere else.

Then he became preoccupied with the wheel again. He saw his life as the wheel's track printed on the desert, left behind by that inexorable and monstrous onward rolling. He wanted to make the lion understand that the wheel that forever bore the unscathed king away from him bore the king away from himself as well. However many wheels there were, there was in reality only one wheel. The wheel on the cage-wagon that brought the lion to the place of his death was the chariot wheel that hurried the king to his own death farther on its track. There was only one wheel, and nothing and no one had power against it.

Jachin-Boaz took another copy of the art book from the stockroom and looked at it several times during the afternoon. Often he was on the verge of weeping. He wanted to buy the book, but thought of the cost of beefsteak and borrowed it instead. When the shop closed he hurried home with the book, stopping on the way to buy meat.

At the butcher's he looked at the carcases hanging on hooks, stared at their nakedness.

All evening he sat at his desk, silent with the book before him, looking at the picture of the lion biting the wheel. Gretel had come to know his moods by now and was accustomed to them. She did not ask Jachin-Boaz why he had particular expressions on his face at certain times.

He knew that he would go out to meet the lion before dawn. He felt like a condemned man, and was surprised to find that he wanted to make love. There were times when it seemed to him that the different parts of him were not all under the same management.

Afterwards he lay looking at the glow in the night sky over the city. He fell asleep, dreamed that he was running on an enormous master-map with the bronze-studded tyre of the chariot wheel rolling behind him, scraping his back, tearing flesh from his back as it pursued him.

At half-past four he woke up remembering nothing of his dream, bathed, shaved, dressed, and went out carrying the meat for the lion.

Jachin-Boaz saw the lion as soon as he came out of the

building. He was lying on the pavement across the street, the light from the overhead lamp making harsh black shadows under the frowning brows.

He knows now that I know who he is, thought Jachin-Boaz. We are countrymen. Jachin-Boaz's legs became weak, and there was coldness in the pit of his stomach. He wanted and did not want to go towards the lion, and he felt his body advancing while his mind sat like a passenger inside his head, looking out through his eyes and seeing the lion grow larger as the distance between them lessened.

The lighted red telephone kiosk was only a few yards to his left, and he moved in that direction as he walked diagonally towards the lion. When the telephone kiosk was ten feet away and the lion was twenty feet in front of him Jachin-Boaz stopped. Again he smelled the hot sun, the dry wind, the lion-smell.

The lion got slowly to his feet, stood watching him. He *was* thin, Jachin-Boaz saw.

Jachin-Boaz moved forward a little farther, threw the meat to the lion. The lion pounced, tore at the meat as he held it between his paws, ate it quickly, growling. He licked his chops, looked at Jachin-Boaz, his eyes like steady green fires.

'Lion,' Jachin-Boaz heard himself say, 'we are countrymen, you and I.' His voice seemed loud in the empty street. He looked up at the dark windows of the flats behind the lion. 'Lion,' he said, 'you have come out of the darkness into which the wheel took you. What do you want?'

For answer his mind showed him lion-coloured desert, singing silence in the heat of the sun, taloned sunlight opening endlessly in the eyes of his mind, lion-sunlight, golden rage, blackness.

'Lion,' said Jachin-Boaz. He was humbled by the lion-feeling his mind had given him, he was dominated by the lion's commanding presence, found it difficult to go on. 'Lion,' he said, 'who am I that I should speak to you? You are a king among lions, I see that plainly. I am not a king among men. I am not your equal.' While he spoke he watched the lion's face, his feet, his tail. He kept his eyes on the lighted telephone kiosk and edged a little closer to it.

'But it is you, lion, who have sought me out,' he continued. 'I did not seek you.' He paused as he heard himself say that. The lion had come out of the wheel's turning darkness. Had not he, Jachin-Boaz, entered that darkness, seeking with his map?

The sky was paling quickly. As on the first morning, a crow flapped slowly overhead, settled on a chimney pot. Perhaps the same crow. Jachin-Boaz, thinking of the turning darkness from which the lion had come, wanted to close his eyes and enter it, but was afraid to.

Then words imprinted themselves on his mind, large, powerful, compelling belief and respect like the saying of a god in capital letters:

TO CLOSE ONE'S EYES IN THE PRESENCE OF A LION

He felt, as in a dream, the layered meanings of the words that stood upright in his mind as if carved in the stone of a temple.

Jachin-Boaz closed his eyes, felt the darkness slowly rise up in him, felt its turning endlessly revolving through him, rested on its constant motion. He saw sunlight in his mind again, rich patterns of colour mottled with falling gold, sunlight as on oriental carpets.

He remembered the darkness with a smile. Yes, he thought comfortably in the sunlight, turning always. One way. No way back. The blackness surged up through the sunlight, bright with terror, snaky, brilliant. One way. No way back.

I shall cease to exist at any moment, he thought. No more world. No more me.

He dropped through blackness, sank through time to green-lit ooze and primal salt, to green light through the reeds. Being, he sensed, is. Goes on. Trust in being. He rested there, prostrate in his mind, awaiting his ascent.

From the green light and the salt he rose, opened his eyes. The lion had not moved.

'My lord Lion,' said Jachin-Boaz. 'I trust in being. I trust in you. I fear you and I am glad that you exist. Respectfully I speak to you, and who am I that I should speak?

'I am Jachin-Boaz, trader in maps, maker of maps. I am the son of Boaz-Jachin, trader in maps before me. I am the father of Boaz-Jachin, who now sits in the shop where I have left him. He has no love for maps, I think, and none perhaps for me.

'Who am I? My father in his coffin lay with his beard pointing like a cannon from his chin. While he lived he praised me and expected much of me. From my early childhood I drew maps of clarity and beauty, much admired. My father and my mother wanted great things from me. For me. Wanted great things for me. Which of course I wanted also.' Jachin-Boaz felt a tightening in his throat — a sound, formed and ready and aching for utterance, a high-pitched single note, a wordless plea. 'Aaaaaaaaaaa-aaaaaaaaa,' he sounded it, a naked, wanting sound. The lion's ears went back.

'They wanted,' said Jachin-Boaz. 'I wanted. Two wantings. Not the same. No. Not the same.'

The lion crouched quietly, the green-fire eyes fixed always on Jachin-Boaz's face.

'What is the sound of not wanting, my lord Lion?'

The lion rose to his feet and roared. The sound filled the street like a river in flood, a great river of lion-coloured sound. From his time, from the tawny running on the plains, from the pit and the fall and the oblong of blue sky overhead, from his death on the spears in the dry wind forward into all the darknesses and lights revolving to the morning light above the city and the river with its bridges the lion sent his roar.

Jachin-Boaz swam in the river of the sound, walked in the valley of it, walked towards the lion and the eyes now amber in the morning.

'Lion,' he said, 'Brother Lion! Boaz-Jachin's lion, blessed anger of my son and golden rage! But you are more than that. You are of me and my lost son both, and of my father and me lost to each other for ever. You are of all of us, Lion.' He moved closer, a heavy taloned paw flashed out and knocked him off his feet. He rolled upright, fell towards the telephone kiosk and was inside it closing the door, waiting for the shattering of glass, the heavy paw and its talons and the open jaws of death. He fainted.

When consciousness returned to Jachin-Boaz the sun was shining. His left arm hurt terribly. He saw that his sleeve hung in blood-soaked shreds, his arm was bloody, there was blood on the floor of the telephone kiosk. Blood still ran from the long deep cuts of the lion's claws. His watch was smashed, stopped at half-past five.

He opened the door. The lion was gone. There was very little movement in the street, nobody waiting at the bus stop. It must still be early morning, he thought as he staggered back to the flat leaving a trail of blood behind him.

He had wanted to tell the lion about the wheel, and he realized now that he had forgotten it completely.

# 16

It was evening, and Boaz-Jachin was still on the road. In the last town he had stopped at he had earned a little money playing his guitar and singing, had bought some bread and cheese, and had slept in the square. I can always get through every night into the morning, he had thought while sitting on a bench looking at the stars.

Now he was tired, and the twilight seemed a lonelier time than night. Always the road, said the twilight. Always the fading of the day. The look of moving headlights on the evening road under a sky still light made Boaz-Jachin's throat ache. He remembered how there used to be a house he slept in every night, and a father and mother.

An old dented van, puttering unevenly, petrol-and-farm smelling, slowed down and stopped beside him. The driver was a young man with a rough unshaven face, squinting.

He leaned out of the window, looked at the guitar-case, looked at Boaz-Jachin, cleared his throat.

'You know any of the old songs?' he said.

'Which ones?' said Boaz-Jachin.

'*The Well*?' said the farmer. He hummed the tune off-key. 'The girl is at the well waiting for her lover and he doesn't come. How many times will she fill her jug? say the old women in the square. And the girl laughs and says the vessel will not be filled until there comes to her that young man with his smiling face ... '

'I know it,' said Boaz-Jachin. He sang the refrain:

Black is the olive, black are his eyes,
Sweet are his kisses, sweeter his lies,
Dark is the water, deep is the well,
Who will give tomorrow's kisses none can tell.

'That's it,' said the farmer. 'Also *The Orange Grove?*'

'Yes,' said Boaz-Jachin. 'I know that one too.'

'Where are you going?' said the farmer.

'The port.'

'Take you another day at least. You want to earn some money? I'll drive you to the port afterwards.'

'How do I earn the money?' said Boaz-Jachin.

'Making music for my father,' said the farmer. 'Singing songs. He's dying.' He opened the door, Boaz-Jachin got in, the van started up.

'Tractor went over him, smashed him all up,' said the farmer. 'He'd stopped on a slope, forgot to put the hand-brake on, got down to fix the harrow hitch. Tractor rolled back on him. He's all smashed up. Wheel went right over him, broke half his ribs and he's got a punctured lung. He was haemorrhaging inside for a long time before anybody went out to look for him.

'It's his own goddam fault. He never had his mind on what he was doing any more. All right. So that's how it is. He'll hear the songs Benjamin used to sing and he'll die and that'll be that.

'By now he can't talk, you understand. He's lying there having a big struggle just to breathe. Can't move his right arm at all. With his left arm, with a finger of his left hand, he makes on the table the name *Benjamin*. Benjamin I can't give him. I figure I'll give him at least the songs. Maybe he won't know the difference. Son of a bitch.' He began to cry.

My second crying driver, thought Boaz-Jachin. 'Who's Benjamin?' he said.

'My brother,' said the farmer. 'He went away ten years ago, when he was sixteen. We never heard from him again.'

He turned off into a bumpy dirt road. The headlights looked at stones and dirt, the sound of crickets came in through the open windows. There was cow dung on the road, pastures on either side, the smell of cows. The sparse grass, pale in the headlights, seemed to have been dragged unwilling from the earth blade by blade.

The van bumped and jolted until there were lighted windows ahead, went in through a gate, pulled up by a shed with a corrugated metal roof. There was a barn behind it, a house to one side. The house was squarish and ugly, made of cement blocks with a tiled roof. In the doorway, silhouetted against the light, stood a woman, a bulky dark figure.

'Is he still alive?' said the farmer.

'Certainly he's still alive,' she said. 'He's been dying already for quite a few years. Why should he rush the job now just because a tractor ran over him? Who's this? You decided this is a good time to bring company home for dinner, or you're opening a youth hostel?'

'I thought, let him hear some music,' said the farmer.

'Wonderful,' said the mother. 'That'll cheer everybody up. We'll have a nervous breakdown together while your father dies. With ideas like this you should work in a resort, a hotel. You should be a social director.'

'Would you feel better if we stood out here all night or may we come in?' said the farmer.

'Come in, welcome, have a good time, enjoy yourselves,' said the mother. She left the doorway and went into the kitchen.

'Probably our guest wouldn't say no to something to eat,' the farmer called after his mother.

'Anything you want,' she said. 'Twenty-four hours a day. Serving you is my supreme joy.'

The farmer and Boaz-Jachin sat down in a parlour with ugly pictures on the walls, a bowl of fruit on a sideboard, a short-wave radio, some books, some ugly vases. The spaces between things in the room separated them rather than connected them.

'Maybe we better have a look, see what kind of shape he's in,' said the farmer. 'If he's dead it's no use singing for him.' He got up, led the way upstairs. Boaz-Jachin followed with his guitar, looking at his back, the frayed shirt with the sweat dried into it, the heavy dragging trousers with a rusty bolt sticking out of one pocket, a coil of wire in another.

'Even if he's dead it might be nice for him to have a song,' said Boaz-Jachin. 'If nobody would mind.'

Upstairs the father lay in a strong dark bed while the room stood up around him. The chairs stood up, the wallpaper stood up, the windows stood up in the wall, the night stood up outside the windows.

A chromium-plated pole with a crossbar stood up beside the bed, a plastic bottle hung on a hook from the bar, a plastic tube fed the big vein in the father's arm.

There were white bandages across his chest and over his right shoulder. The skin of his neck and chest that was usually exposed by his collar opening was creased and dark and weathered. Elsewhere the skin was white and in-experienced-looking. His eyes were closed, his head lay back on the pillow, his beard pointed like a cannon from his chin. His breath whistled in and out, fluttered, broke, went on unevenly.

His wrist, coloured like his neck, came out of his thin white arm, presented itself as the wrist of a boy. Forget the years, said the wrist. This is how I used to lie on the coverlet

83

when someone else was the man and I was the boy. I had nothing in my hand then, I have nothing in my hand now.

The doctor sat in a chair by the bed. He wore a dark suit, open sandals over dark socks, looked at his watch, looked at the father's face.

'The hospital's twenty miles away,' said the farmer to Boaz-Jachin. 'The ambulance was out, couldn't get here for hours. The doctor came, did what he could right here, said not to move him now.'

The farmer looked at the doctor, pointed to Boaz-Jachin's guitar.

The doctor looked at the father's face, nodded.

The mother came in with coffee, fruit and cheese, while Boaz-Jachin tuned his guitar. She poured coffee for the doctor, for her son and Boaz-Jachin, then sat in a straight-backed chair, her hands in her lap.

Boaz-Jachin played and sang *The Well*:

> By the well in the square
> See her waiting daily there ...

The sound of the guitar, round and expanding, moved out from him to the standing-up walls, came back into the centre of the room, said to the walls, Not you. Beyond you.

The father's breath whistled in and out unevenly the same as before. When Boaz-Jachin sang the refrain the mother walked to the window and stood before her reflection on the night:

> Dark is the water, deep is the well,
> Who will give tomorrow's kisses none can tell.

Boaz-Jachin sang *The Orange Grove*:

> Where the morning sees the shadows
> Of the orange grove, there was nothing
> twenty years ago.

Where the dry wind sowed the desert
We brought water, planted seedlings, now
    the oranges grow.

'Did you bring in the tractor?' said the mother to the son.
'It's in the shed,' he said. 'His eyes are open.'

The father's eyes, large and black, looked straight up at the ceiling. His left hand was moving on the bedside table.

The son stood over his father's moving hand, watched the finger spelling on the dark wood of the night table.

'F-O-R ... ' he read. The finger kept moving. ' "Forgive," ' said the son.

'Always the humorist,' said the mother.

'Benjamin he forgives,' said the son. 'Always.'

'Maybe he meant you,' said the doctor.

'Maybe he's asking,' said Boaz-Jachin. 'For himself.'

Everyone turned to look at him while the father died. When they looked back at the father there was no sound of breathing, the eyes were closed, the hand on the table was still.

Boaz-Jachin spent the night in the room that had been Benjamin's. In the morning the mother made the funeral arrangements and the son drove Boaz-Jachin to the port.

They travelled all day, stopping halfway for lunch in a café. The son had shaved and was wearing a suit and a sports shirt. It was evening when they came to the port. The sky showed that they were at the sea.

They went down steep cobbled streets towards the water, came to the open cobbled quayside of the harbour, and cafés with red and yellow light-bulbs strung outside. Lights of ships and boats tied up at piers and lights of quayside buildings were reflected in the water.

The farmer took folded money from his pocket.

'No, please,' said Boaz-Jachin. 'There shouldn't be money

between us. You gave me something, I gave you something.'

They shook hands, the van pulled away, climbed the cobbled streets back to the road away from the port.

Later, when Boaz-Jachin marked his map, he found that he had only the name *Benjamin* to give to that family.

# 17

Jachin-Boaz had fainted again when he got to the flat. Gretel called an ambulance, and he was carried to it on a stretcher.

At the hospital admitting office Jachin-Boaz said that he had fallen against a spiked fence while drunk. He told the same thing to the nurse who cleaned his wounds when she questioned him. When the doctor came to sew up the worst cuts he too asked how Jachin-Boaz had got them.

'Spiked fence,' said Jachin-Boaz.

'Yes,' said the doctor. 'It seems to have lashed out at you with tremendous speed and force. Dragged its spikes right down your arm too. One wants to be careful about provoking fences like that.'

'Yes,' said Jachin-Boaz. He was afraid that he would be locked up as a lunatic if the truth were found out.

'It didn't happen to be a spiked fence near the tiger cages at the zoo, did it?' said the doctor.

'I didn't see any tiger cages when it happened,' said Jachin-Boaz. For all he knew there could be heavy fines involved, revocation of his work permit, even his passport. But certainly no one could prove that he had been interfering with the tigers.

'I suppose in your country they have a certain number of strange cults, strange rites,' said the doctor.

'I am an atheist,' said Jachin-Boaz. 'I have no rites.'

While the doctor stitched up Jachin-Boaz's wounds an orderly called the zoo to enquire whether there had been any disturbances having to do with tigers, leopards, or other large felines. The zoo had nothing to report.

'I shouldn't be surprised if he was wearing an amulet of some kind,' said the doctor after Jachin-Boaz had gone, 'but I didn't think to look. They come into this country and they take advantage of the National Health Service, but they cling to the old ways among their own.'

The orderly said to his wife that evening at dinner, 'There are things going on at the zoo that the ordinary citizen knows nothing of.'

'Among the animals?' said his wife.

'Animals and people — how much difference is there if it comes to that?' said the orderly. 'Cults, sex orgies, the lot. Our immigration policy wants a good overhauling, and that's the long and short of it. Our way of life can't stand up to this foreign influx indefinitely.'

'But foreign animals, you know,' said his wife. 'What's a zoo without them? Think how the children would miss them.'

Gretel and Jachin-Boaz both stayed home from work that day. Jachin-Boaz rested in bed, his arm wrapped in white bandages. Gretel looked after him with soup, peppermint tea, brandy, custards, strudel. She cooked and baked all day, thumping and banging in the kitchen and singing in her own language.

When Jachin-Boaz had come home all bloody that morning he had fainted without an explanation, and in the ambulance had begged to be excused from going into the matter just then. Gretel had become aware of his early-morning departures from the flat, but she had said nothing. If he needed to go out at quarter to five every morning she would not question it. She had been terrified by his bloody return this morning, had listened, unquestioning, to his spiked-fence story at the hospital, and continued to ask no questions. Her no-question-asking stalked through the flat like a tall silent creature that stared at Jachin-Boaz all day.

For most of the day Jachin-Boaz could do nothing but concentrate all his energies on holding himself together. The snaky black and brilliant panic that had surged up in him when he had closed his eyes in the presence of the lion had torn away the sodden rotting cover from a well of terror in him, and into that well his mind dropped like an echoing stone.

He cowered under the covers, hugging himself and shivering with a chill that soup and brandy and peppermint tea could not take away. When he look around the room his eyes could not take in sufficient light. The day, however it varied from sunny to grey, had less than normal light in it. The twilight was appalling. The lamps when lit seemed feeble, unavailing. His terror stood up strong in him while he lay down. What brought him back to here-and-now was worrying about more beafsteak for the lion.

'Will you be doing any shopping later?' he asked Gretel casually.

'I did quite a bit of shopping yesterday,' she said. 'There's nothing we need unless you want me to get something for you.'

'No,' said Jachin-Boaz. 'I'm fine. Thank you anyway.' He began mentally to rehearse different ways of mentioning seven pounds of beefsteak. He couldn't say, You might pick up seven pounds of beef at the butcher's. He couldn't send her out three times for two pounds of beef and once more for one pound. He couldn't go out and come back with it inconspicuously or in defiant silence.

While he deliberated Gretel was in and out of the bedroom, the living room, the kitchen, filling the flat with domestic sounds, singing incomprehensibly, bringing him coffee, chocolate bars, cleaning, dusting. His silence rose up in him like a pillar of stone while her no-question-asking stalked in and out with her, looking over her shoulder and staring.

After a time Jachin-Boaz said in a strained voice, 'We're good together, you and I. These months have been good ones.'

'Yes,' said Gretel, thinking, Now it comes: bad news.

'We can be together, but we can also be alone with each other,' said Jachin-Boaz, 'each with privacy, one's own thoughts.'

'Yes,' said Gretel. Who could be after him? she thought. Brothers of his wife? With knives? What kind of cuts were those on his arm? Not knives.

'We can tell each other everything, every kind of thing,' said Jachin-Boaz. 'And also we can allow each other to have things that are not told.'

'Yes,' said Gretel. Not his wife's brothers perhaps, she thought. The brothers of some other woman? Some other woman herself? I'm eighteen years younger than he is. Is she younger than I am? Prettier?

'If I asked you to go out and buy seven pounds of beef-steak and not ask me why, would you do it?' said Jachin-Boaz.

'Yes,' said Gretel.

'Thank you,' said Jachin-Boaz. 'Take money from my wallet. It's on the desk.' He sighed, feeling relaxed and sleepy. Would he, wouldn't he, go out to meet the lion tomorrow morning? He would think about it later when he woke up before dawn.

Jachin-Boaz took a nap. He dreamed of a lion-coloured plain and himself walking slowly across it with nothing in sight. From the silence behind him he heard a whispering rolling that grew louder, brazen and heavy.

He knew without turning to look that it was the wheel,

and the urge to escape became gigantic in him, too big for his body. He could not convert the urge to action because the vastness of the space made running impossible. There was no place to escape to. There was only empty timeless space all around him under a flat blue sky, and he continued to walk slowly while the escape-urge leaped up in him as if it would burst his throat.

The wheel was closer, the sound greater, filling all the emptiness of the plain. Jachin-Boaz felt the studded bronze tyre on his back, crushing him, printing its track upon him, passing over him but not going on, not going away. Again it approached from behind, clamorous with voices, and on its rim now, turning with it, were the coffins of his father and his mother.

The wheel went over him again, splintering the coffins, pressing the bodies into his own body – his father's maleness, his mother's belly and breasts that now became those of his wife, and it was her body on the wheel crushing him. He turned and clung to her, face to face and front to naked front as the wheel crushed him. It's all right, he thought. This is the way back, the wheel will take me back. The world won't go away now. There'll be world and me again.

He looked up as the wheel passed over him, saw it pass beyond him, saw spears fly over his head into his son Boaz-Jachin who already had two arrows in him and was leaping up at the wheel.

'No more other,' said Jachin-Boaz. No more great dark shoulder-world-wheel turning away. He laughed and felt his naked mother warm above him. 'It's all right now,' he said as she opened her scissor-legs and brought her weight down on him. The blades enclosed his penis as he thrust, safe and cosy, deep into his wife. 'World again, me again,' he said. 'No more other.'

He woke up with Gretel lying partly on him, her head on

his chest. Her tears were wet on his skin. How am I here? Who is she? he thought as he kissed her wet face. What am I doing with her? He remembered nothing of his dream. In his mind was a memory of Sunday drives when he sat between his father and his mother, watching the waning sunlight with dread. He always got carsick on those drives.

Gretel cooked dinner and brought it in on a tray. Jachin-Boaz sat up in bed, eating and wondering how he had got to this place and this girl. Gretel sat on the edge of the bed with her plate on her lap and ate in silence.

That night Jachin-Boaz slept well, and he awoke at the usual time. In the dimness of the morning he walked into the living room, to his desk and the master-map spread on it.

Jachin-Boaz ran his finger over the smooth paper. If he poked sharply his finger would make a hole in the map, go through it and come out on the other side without having penetrated anything but the thickness of the paper. So his life seemed now: he could poke himself through the flat paper of the map-city he walked on and he would come out on the other side, having only made a hole in non-reality.

Jachin-Boaz spoke to the map. 'The man says to the place, "What will you give me?"'

'The place says, "Take whatever you want."'

'The man says, "What do I want?"'

'The place has no answer for him.'

'The place asks a question in its turn, "Why are you here?"'

'The man looks away and cannot speak.' Jachin-Boaz touched the map again, then turned away.

He was out in the street with the beefsteak in his carrier-bag before five o'clock. It was dark and rainy, and only when he saw the glistening street was he aware that he seemed to have decided to meet the lion again. Will the lion be wet too? he wondered.

The lion too was wet and glistening. The lion-smell was

stronger in the rain. Jachin-Boaz threw him the meat immediately, and the lion ate it, growling. With his bandaged arm Jachin-Boaz felt a little easier than before with the lion, felt comradely with him, as if they had both fought on the same side in a war.

'Comrade Lion,' he said. He liked the sound of that. 'Comrade Lion, you will kill me or you will not kill me. Your frown is the frown I have seen on the face of my son and on the face of my father. Perhaps it is also the one I see in the mirror. Come, let's walk a little.'

Jachin-Boaz turned his back on the lion and walked towards the river. He went along the embankment, looking back to see if the lion was following. He was. What does he see? Jachin-Boaz wondered. Does he see only me? Is everything else not there?

He walked past the first bridge to the second with the lion following, walked up the steps and on to the bridge, looking up at the cables and the dark sky, feeling the rain on his face. At the middle he stopped, leaned his back against the parapet. The lion stopped ten feet away and stood with his head lifted, watching him.

'Doctor Lion,' said Jachin-Boaz, 'my father used to look at the maps I drew and say that I would be a man of science. But he was wrong. I never became a man of science. The money that he spent on my education was wasted.' He laughed, and the lion crouched. 'I am alive and he is dead, and the money was wasted.

'He used to say, "I can tell by the way he writes, the way he draws, his exactitude, his sense of order, the questions he asks, that this boy will be a scientist. He will not sit in a shop waiting for customers to jingle the bell."

'One day when I was still a little boy, still playing with toy guns, he brought home for me two presents to choose between. One was a western cowboy suit, like those worn in the films, splendid in black and silver, with a sombrero, with a leather waistcoat, with great flapping leather trousers with silver bosses, with a cartridge belt and two shining pistols in black and silver holsters.

'The other was a microscope and a box of scientific equipment and materials — slides, test tubes, beakers, retorts, graduates, chemicals, a book of experiments. "Choose," he told me.

'I wanted the black-and-silver leather, the sombrero, the shining pistols. I chose the microscope and the test tubes. Are you looking at your watch, Doctor Lion? The sky is dark, but it is almost daytime now.'

Jachin-Boaz walked towards the lion. The lion backed away, growling. Jachin-Boaz shouted, 'I TOLD YOU OF SOMETHING THAT I WANTED ONCE. ARE YOU BORED, LION? ONCE I CLEARLY WANTED SOMETHING, NOT A VERY BIG THING. IS YOUR TIME TOO VALUABLE FOR YOU TO LISTEN ANY LONGER?'

The lion had turned his back on Jachin-Boaz, and now walked off the bridge, down the steps, and was out of sight behind the parapet of the embankment.

Jachin-Boaz followed. When he got to the embankment there was no lion. Only the rain, the pavement and the street wet and glistening, the hiss of tyres on the road.

'YOU WEREN'T LISTENING!' shouted Jachin-Boaz to the empty air, the rain. 'THERE WAS A TIME WHEN I WANTED SOMETHING AND I KNEW WHAT IT WAS. I WANTED A BLACK-AND-SILVER COWBOY SUIT WITH TWO PISTOLS.'

'Cheer up, mate,' said the police constable with whom Jachin-Boaz collided while going down the steps. 'Perhaps Father Christmas'll bring you one. You've plenty of time till December.'

94

# 18

Boaz-Jachin walked on the quayside in the darkness beyond the lights of the cafés. Above the harbour were the honey-combed lights of the big new hotel, and behind it the coloured lights and smoky flames of the oil refinery. Sometimes the wind brought dance music down from the hotel. The jukebox music from the cafés had darkness all around it, like the red and yellow bulbs strung outside. Boaz-Jachin did not want to go into the cafés. He did not want to play his guitar again for money just yet.

He walked out on to a pier between boats tied up on either side, creaking at their mooring lines while the water of the harbour slapped at their sides. Some showed lights, some were dark. Across the water at the harbour mouth the light on the mole turned and flashed. Boaz-Jachin smelled fish and sour wine, the salt-wood smell of boats, the harbour-water quietly slapping piles and planking.

He smelled petrol, oranges, and orange-crate wood, and thought of the lorry driver. The smell was coming from a boat with lights in the wheelhouse and cabin skylight. The boat was broad-beamed and big-bellied and painted blue, with a stumpy mast forward, the sail loosely furled on a short boom. Automobile tyres hung along its sides. The high bow curved back on itself with certain classical pre-tensions, was ornamented with two blind bulging wooden eyes, and sported an archaic anchor. A blue dinghy was tied up astern.

I'm the real thing, said the backward-curving bow, the wooden eyes, the archaic anchor: brown-faced men squinting into the morning fog, women in black waiting. Maybe the sea and I will kill you.

Boaz-Jachin walked along the pier the length of the boat, read the name on the stern: *Swallow*. The home port, where the oranges were going, was where he wanted to go. There he could find another boat to take him farther or he could travel overland in the direction of the city where he expected to find his father.

He sat down on the string-piece, took out his guitar, and played *The Orange Grove* without singing the words, thinking of the desert in the song that was far from the sea, the sparse green of the grass at the farm of the Benjamin family.

A man came out of the *Swallow*'s wheelhouse and leaned against it, his face mostly in shadow. He wore a wrinkled dark suit, a wrinkled white shirt with no tie, and pointed dark shoes. He looked like a rumpled waiter.

'Nice,' said the man. 'A nice song. Sounds good, music like that coming over the water.'

'Thank you,' said Boaz-Jachin.

'I see you looking at the boat,' said the man. 'She's a sweet one, this one, eh? Catches the eye. *Swallow*, her name is. Over the waves like a bird. Comes from the other side. Here they don't build them like this.'

Boaz-Jachin nodded. He knew nothing about boats, but this one looked slow, burdensome, heavy. 'Do you sail her or has she got an engine?' he said.

'Engine,' said the man. 'The sail is just to keep her steady. She used to be rigged for sail when my father was alive. Not now. Too much fucking trouble. This way I get there, I get back, I have a good time ashore, no trouble. I come over with wine and cheese, I go back with oranges, melons, whatever. You're on your way somewhere, right? You're going somewhere. Where are you going?'

'Where you're taking the oranges,' said Boaz-Jachin.

'You're hanging around looking for a boat. You're hoping maybe you can work your way across,' said the trader. When the light at the harbour mouth flashed and turned one side of his face was lit up. He had a big smile, large teeth, looked desperate.

'I had a feeling when I saw you,' said the trader. 'Sometimes it's like that — you see a person, get a feeling. I'll make a bet with you: I'll bet you've never been on a boat before, you don't know how to steer, you can't cook, and if I told you to cast off the mooring lines you wouldn't know which rope to put your hand to.'

'That's right,' said Boaz-Jachin.

'That's what I thought,' said the trader. Again a big smile. 'It's all right. You're in luck anyhow, because my cousin isn't coming back with me this trip. You can help me take her over. I'll show you how to steer, and all you have to do is keep awake.'

'All right,' said Boaz-Jachin. 'Thank you.'

'We'll go out in the morning,' said the trader. 'You can sleep on board.'

The bunks were below, next to the galley, and smelled of petrol, salt wood, tobacco smoke, and old frying. Boaz-Jachin took a blanket and lay down on deck, watching the stars, large and bright, rocking above him. Between him and the stars the beam of the harbour light swept as it turned. He fell asleep thinking of Lila and the night they had slept on the roof of her house.

In the morning he was awakened by the sun on his face. There was a professional-looking seagull perching on the mast. It looked down at Boaz-Jachin with a contemptuous yellow eye that said, I'm ready for business and you're still asleep. Other gulls were flying over the harbour with creaking cries, screaming over the garbage behind the cafés, perching on masts and piles.

The trader treated Boaz-Jachin to coffee and rolls at one of the cafés. Then he took on fuel, cleared his cargo at the harbourmaster's shack, hoisted the steadying sail and started the engine. Towing her dinghy astern the *Swallow* puttered past freighters and tankers from whose galleys came the clink of cups and the smell of coffee. Here and there men in shorts or pyjamas leaned on railings looking down, standing in the morning shadows that moved slowly in the sunlight on the metal decks. This is life, thought Boaz-Jachin. This is being out in the world.

They cleared the harbour mouth, passed the old stone mole with its lighthouse now standing sleepy like an owl in strong sunlight, and went out past the channel markers, heading into a fresh wind from the west and a slight chop outside. The sunlight danced in glints and sparkles on the green water. The gull, still on the masthead, expressed with his eye that it was a late start but never mind.

The trader was still wearing his pointed shoes, his dark suit trousers, and his wrinkled white shirt, now more wrinkled and less white, but no jacket. The boat pitched slowly as she went, her big-bellied hull pounding in the chop. The sunlight glinted on the little brass wheel as the trader handled the spokes.

'She pounds, eh?' he said. 'She's not built for an engine, the old bitch. Built for sail. With an engine it's like driving a big heavy pancake over a bumpy road. Wears you out.'

'Why don't you sail her?' said Boaz-Jachin.

'Because she's motorized now,' said the trader. He seemed almost angry. 'She's not rigged for sail any more. This is not the old days. My old man used to keep me hopping. One of these things rigged for sail, you've got two masts, big long yards. Every time you go about you have to dip the yard, bring it around the other side of the mast, set everything up again on the weather side. Big sailing deal. "Move, boy!

Hop!" I can still hear him. Big deal sailor, my old man. Fuck that. This is modern times, eh? He was a wonderful man.' The trader spat to leeward from the wheelhouse window. 'Sail like the devil, afraid of nothing. Great pilot. You never saw anything like it. Knew where he was anytime. Middle of the darkest night, no land, no nothing, knew where he was.'

'How do you know where you are when you're out of sight of land?' said Boaz-Jachin. He saw nothing scientific-looking in the wheelhouse but the compass and the fuel and engine gauges. No instruments that looked like navigation.

The trader showed him a wooden board in which were drilled many little holes in the thirty-two-spoked wheel of a compass rose. Below that were short vertical lines of holes. Pegs, attached to the board by strings, were in some of the holes.

'When I need to I use this,' he said. 'Every point of the compass is divided into half-hours. I mark with a peg how long I've been on any heading. Down below I mark the speed. I add on or take off for wind and current with me or against me, and that's how I know where I am. That's how my father did it, and I do it the same.'

'I thought you had to have instruments, charts, maps, take sights and all that,' said Boaz-Jachin.

'That's a lot of crap for playboys with yachts,' said the trader. 'I know the winds, the currents, the bottom, I know where I am. What do I need all that machinery for? My father was the best sailor, the best pilot out of our port. Fifteen, twenty other men masters of their own boats in our village, but if you came there a stranger and asked for "the Captain" they knew you meant him, nobody else. From him I learned the sea.'

'You had a good father,' said Boaz-Jachin.

The trader nodded, spat again through the wheelhouse

window. 'Nobody like him,' he said, and sighed. ' "Keep the boat and follow the sea," he told me. Left it to me in his will. So here I am. This trip oranges, next one wine, cheese, olives, whatever. It's not a bad life, eh? I mean it's a proper thing for a man to do—not like running a restaurant or some shore thing like that. Dressed up like a gentleman all the time, greeting your clientele, making them feel big by remembering their names. White tablecloths, flowers, snapping your fingers for the wine waiter. A mural on the wall with the bay and the grottoes. All the same, for some people that too is a way of life. Takes all kinds, eh?'

'Yes,' said Boaz-Jachin, 'I guess it does.'

'That's how it is,' said the trader. 'For me, as for my father, it's the sea. Always the other thing looks good, you know—the thing you don't have, the road you didn't take.' He put his arm out through the window, slapped the side of the wheelhouse. '*Swallow*'s all right,' he said. 'She's all right.'

The coast slid by—stretches of brown, stretches of green, old red rocks, lion-coloured cliffs, ruined forts, oil tanks, water tanks, pipelines. Blocks and planes and facets of houses, roofs, walls, angles scattering down hillsides, each casting a morning shadow. White walls, red tile roofs, black-cut windows and doorways. Clusters of boats painted blue, painted white. Boats in twos and threes, single boats passing. Sometimes a tanker, sometimes a big white cruise ship. The gull flew off the masthead as the *Swallow* left the coast astern and headed out to sea. The salt wind had a deep-water smell.

'Where are we on the chart?' said Boaz-Jachin towards the afternoon. There was no land in sight.

'I don't have a chart,' said the trader. 'A chart's a picture. Why bother with a picture of the ocean when you've got the ocean to read? We're half a day out from the port we left and we're two days away from the port we're bound for. Keep her on this heading while I make some lunch.'

Boaz-Jachin, alone in the wheelhouse for the first time, suddenly felt the weight of the sea that *Swallow* pounded through, the depth and the weight of it heaving against the boat's old bottom. The engine chugged steadily, driving her on. She answered the wheel easily as he gave or took a spoke, his eye on the quivering compass card. Ahead of him the sunlight on the water danced, and dancing light reflected from the water rippled on the wheelhouse ceiling like flashes of mystic writing, like word-flashes in an unknown language. The blue dinghy followed astern like a child of the boat, its bows slapping the water in the wake of the *Swallow*, its own smaller wake spreading briefly behind it. Up forward the smoke from the galley stovepipe heat-shimmered against the sky and water, wavered the near and distant images of other boats and ships.

Sometimes Boaz-Jachin saw his face reflected in the wheelhouse windows, recalled the blank face of the king, the frowning face of the lion-king. The being-with-the-lion came back for a moment and was gone again. Again the emptiness, the urge ahead towards something gone out from him.

The chariot wheel, the wheel in his hand ... He felt himself on the verge of understanding something, but could go no farther. He held fast to being where he was.

The trader came on deck with a napkin over his arm, carrying a tray on which was a covered dish, a bottle of wine, a basket of bread, a wine glass, silverware, a clean folded napkin. He set the tray down on the hatch cover, took the napkin from his arm, spread it out, arranged a place setting on it, put the covered dish, the wine bottle, the bread basket in their proper positions, stepped back, looked at everything critically, then came aft to the wheelhouse window.

'The gentleman's table is ready on the terrace now,' he

said. 'I will take the wheel. I ate below before I brought your lunch up.'

There was an omelette under the dish cover, very light and delicate, flavoured with herbs. Boaz-Jachin sat on the hatch cover and ate and drank while the trader watched him from the wheelhouse, smiling his desperate smile and showing his large teeth.

Late in the afternoon the trader took a nap while Boaz-Jachin steered. When he took the helm again he said, 'Tonight we'll stand regular four-hour watches.' In the evening he told Boaz-Jachin to heat a tinned stew and brew a pot of coffee, and he had his dinner in the wheelhouse. 'I'll stay here for a while yet,' he said to Boaz-Jachin. 'You might as well get some sleep.'

When the trader woke Boaz-Jachin it was two o'clock in the morning. Boaz-Jachin looked out through the windows of the dark wheelhouse, saw nothing ahead but the phosphorescence of the bow wave in the blackness of the night. 'Aren't you afraid to leave me alone at the wheel for four hours?' he said. 'What'll I do if something goes wrong?'

'What could go wrong?' said the trader. 'All you have to do is stay awake and keep out of the way of big ships. Our running lights are lit. Here's the switch for the masthead light if you think somebody doesn't see you. Here's the button for the horn. I've showed you how to steer and how to reverse the engine. If you have to relieve yourself you use these two eye-spliced lines on either side to tie down the wheel.'

'How do I stop the boat if I have to?' said Boaz-Jachin. 'For what?'

'I don't know. But if I have to?'

'It's not like an automobile where you can put on the brakes,' said the trader. 'And it's too deep to drop the anchor out here. You have to steer around things or put her in reverse if something shows up in front of you. And if you shut off the engine and let go of the wheel the sail will bring the boat up into the wind and she'll lose way, stop going forward gradually. Right?'

'Right,' said Boaz-Jachin.

The trader looked at his watch, moved some of the pegs in his navigating board, gave Boaz-Jachin a new compass heading. 'In a couple of hours we'll pass a light on the horizon on the starboard side,' he said. After that there's nothing until I come on watch again. All you do is stay on the heading I gave you. Right?'

'Right,' said Boaz-Jachin. The trader went below, and he was alone in the dark wheelhouse with the lighted circle of the compass card and the dim green eyes of the gauges before him. Forward in the blackness the phosphorescent bow wave parted always while the *Swallow*'s wooden eyes looked blindly into the night.

After a time the aloneness became comfortable, the darkness was simply where he was. He remembered the road to the citadel and the ruined palace, how it had seemed nowhere the first time, but the second time it had become the place where he was. The wheel felt good in his hands. When he found his father he would simply say, May I have my map, please? Nothing more than that.

There was a light, a light that turned and flashed from a lighthouse, but it was much closer than the horizon, much sooner than a couple of hours, and it was on the port side.

He said starboard side, thought Boaz-Jachin, and he said it would be on the horizon in a couple of hours. Him and his fucking pegboard. He shut off the engine, let go the wheel, and went below to wake the trader.

'What time is it?' said the trader. 'What happened to the engine?'

'I shut it off,' said Boaz-Jachin. 'It's quarter past three and there's a light on the port side and it's pretty close.'

'Shit,' said the trader, and started for the deck. As he got out of the bunk there was a horrible grating sound along the keel. The boat lifted sharply as they reached the deck, they heard the splintering of planks. The boat lifted again, grated again, with more splintering.

'Get into the dinghy and pull clear,' said the trader in a calm voice to Boaz-Jachin as they half-fell down the slanting deck towards the stern.

Boaz-Jachin, pulling away from the *Swallow* into the darkness, heard the engine start up as the masthead light went on. The *Swallow* leaped glaringly out of the night, the sea lifted her again, she came off the rocks in reverse and started to settle by the bow as the trader jumped clear with a great splash.

My guitar and my map, thought Boaz-Jachin. Gone. By the time the trader had got himself into the dinghy, half swamping it, the masthead light had gone under and they were in darkness again, across which the beam from the lighthouse regularly swept.

'Son of a bitch,' said the trader. 'Son of a bitch.' The sea slapped and gurgled quietly against the dinghy as Boaz-Jachin pulled farther away from the rocks that had sunk the *Swallow*. He could see the trader's hunched shape leaning forward, darker than the sky behind him. Whenever the light swept over them Boaz-Jachin saw his wet white shirt and dark trousers, his face open-mouthed and wet. Suddenly the being-with-the-lion feeling came to Boaz-Jachin. He almost roared. Then it was gone. Emptiness.

'How did I do this to myself?' said the trader quietly. 'How did I find you? What demon possessed me to put my boat in your hands? Mother of God, who sent you to me?'

'You and your fucking pegboard,' said Boaz-Jachin.

'How did that lighthouse get on the wrong side at the wrong time?'

'That's for you to tell me,' said the trader. 'I was sure at least that you could hold a wheel in your hands and look at the compass. When I went below at midnight you were on a safe course. Tell me, you fateful one, imp of the devil, bringer of ill fortune, what did you do then?'

'It wasn't midnight when you went below,' said Boaz-Jachin.

'All right,' said the trader. 'So it was ten past twelve. Not exactly midnight. We're not quite so precise here as in the navy. My humble apologies.'

'It wasn't ten past twelve either,' said Boaz-Jachin. 'I looked at my watch.'

'Don't play games with me, imp,' said the trader. The light swept over them, and Boaz-Jachin saw doubt in his face.

'It was two o'clock in the morning,' said Boaz-Jachin. 'The little hand was at the two and the big hand was at the twelve. If you want to call that ten past twelve, go ahead, do as you like.'

'Ten past twelve is the other way around,' said the trader. 'The little hand, the big hand.'

'Wonderful,' said Boaz-Jachin. 'You're learning fast.'

'Two o'clock in the morning, not ten past twelve,' said the trader. 'We were two hours past where I thought we were when I put you on the new heading.'

'Right,' said Boaz-Jachin. 'Which I stayed on as you told me to, and here we are.'

'Son of a bitch,' said the trader. 'The big hand and the little hand.'

' "Keep the boat and follow the sea," ' said Boaz-Jachin, and he began to laugh.

'I'll tell you something,' said the trader. 'Fuck the sea.

I'll never be able to collect the insurance on *Swallow* because of the way we sank her, but I have a piece of land I can sell, and I'm going to open a restaurant.'

'One thing about a restaurant,' said Boaz-Jachin — 'when you wake up it'll be exactly where it was when you went to sleep.'

'Right,' said the trader. 'So that's that. It's out of my hands. The sea made the decision.'

'Tell me,' said Boaz-Jachin. 'What's the name of the rocks that sank us?'

'The rocks I don't know. The light is Rising Sun Light.'

's-u-n or s-o-n?' said Boaz-Jachin.

's-u-n,' said the trader. 'It faces east.'

'Where the son sank,' said Boaz-Jachin. 'Well, on my new map the rocks will be called Rising Son Rocks, spelled s-o-n. I'm naming them after you.'

'Thank you,' said the trader. 'I'm deeply honoured.'

The sky was pale now, and in the water they saw oranges floating. The trader leaned over and picked up two.

'If the gentleman would like breakfast,' he said, 'his table is now ready.'

# 19

Jachin-Boaz's wife, with her husband and son both gone, now considered the situation in which she found herself. In the first months after Jachin-Boaz's departure she had gone through torments thinking of him in the arms of young and beautiful women. Wherever she looked she seemed to see only girls and young women, all of them so pretty that she wondered how men could choose among them. But she had talked to other women since, and the consensus was that men of her husband's age often did what he had done, that after a few months or a year they yearned for the comforts and habits they had left, and, if allowed to, returned. She was determined to encounter such a possibility from a position of strength. She did not expect her son to come back, and made no effort to trace him. Nor did she attempt to locate his father. She concentrated her energies on the shop. She had long had her own ideas about how to run the business, and now she put them into practice.

She hired a girl to help her. She stocked paperback books, and made lively displays of them in the window. She worked up a line of fortune-telling maps for each sign of the zodiac. She took good-luck charms and cheap jewellery of an occult character on consignment from local craftsmen. She installed a palmist in the parlour above the shop — an elderly lady with jet-black hair and piercing eyes who was clothed entirely in black and turned over to Jachin-Boaz's wife a percentage of whatever she took in. To create an atmosphere around her a coffee machine, tables and chairs were added, and regular coffee-drinkers appeared. A small ensemble of young musicians, playing folk songs and paid by the passing of a basket among the coffee-drinkers, attracted a larger clientele. Soon Jachin-Boaz's wife took in more money in a week than her husband had done in a month.

During business hours she was comfortable, even gay. Sundays were bad. Sundays with Jachin-Boaz had often been depressing. Without him they were frightening. Alone at night she found her thoughts difficult to control. She washed her hair often and took many baths, luxurious with scented soaps and essences, but she avoided looking at her body. She looked at her face often in the mirror and felt unsure of how to compose it, what to do with her mouth. After not having worn her wedding ring for months she put it on, then took it off again. She began to read more than she had for years, and every night took sleeping tablets. Often she dreamed of Jachin-Boaz, and in her waking hours, however she occupied herself, there were thoughts of him most of the time.

Boaz-Jachin was in her mind less often. Sometimes he had seemed a stranger to her. They had not thought alike, had never been as close as she had expected a mother and son to be. Now he seemed less an absent son than an emptiness, an end of something. Sometimes she would be surprised not to hear his footsteps, his guitar, would catch herself thinking of what to cook for him. Sometimes she wondered what he might be doing at a particular moment. His father is in him, she thought. He is lost and wandering, seeking chaos. Sometimes the two of them blurred together in her mind.

She looked at books of poems that Jachin-Boaz had given her when they were young. The inscriptions were full of love and passion. He had found her beautiful and desirable once. She had thought him beautiful, exciting, the young man with whom she would make a green place, a place of strength and achievement. She had sensed greatness in him as a desert-dweller senses water, and she had thirsted for it. She had fallen in love with him, and she had locked herself in the bathroom and cried because she knew that he would give her pain.

Jachin-Boaz and she had met at university. She was in the arts course, he was reading natural sciences, a brilliant scholar. Then unaccountably he had failed his examinations, had left university to work in his father's shop. Soon after that the father had died. Then she too had left university, and they had married, living with Jachin-Boaz's mother above the shop for what seemed long years while the mother throve in chronic ill health until struck down by a bus. If not for that bus she would still be here, thought Jachin-Boaz's wife, surrounded by her medicines, telling me how to take care of her son, telling me what a wonderful life they had when the father was alive, telling me what a wonderful husband the father had been, not telling me about the mistress that everybody knew about but her. Did she know? The wonderful husband. Another one like my father with his green place in the desert. The good place is never here, the man's heart is never here.

When Jachin-Boaz's mother had died his wife had expected him to emerge into a new life. She had never abandoned the conviction she had when she had fallen in love with him that he would be a famous scientist. She had always felt the seeking-and-finding drive in him, his talent for associating seemingly unrelated data. She knew that she could nurture his gifts and help him to develop them.

With his education incomplete, his start in life delayed, she did not expect him to rise fast and smoothly to eminence, but she was confident that he could find a gentlemanly scientific speciality — beetles it might be, or ancient artifacts

—and on it build a reputation. She imagined letters from fellow scientists all over the world, papers by her husband read at symposia, printed in journals, international visitors drinking coffee, listening to music, talking late into the night, the lamplight warm on a life of culture, of achievement and significance. Jachin-Boaz went on with his work at the shop and found no scientific speciality.

She tried to encourage him to expand and develop the business. He was content with it as it was.

She tried to interest him in a house in the country. He had no interest.

Gone. Nothing. Dry wind in the desert. The pattern of the carpet of her childhood came into her mind, and she shuddered. Here she was. A different carpet. In the square the palm trees rustled in the light of the street lamps. The globes of the lamps were like great blind eyes, the street was empty below the window, a dog trotted past with a black trotting shadow. Here she was and he was gone, the middle-aged man who had turned away from her in bed or made love feebly, made her feel less than a woman, incapable of giving or taking pleasure. And she had seen how he looked at girls. In the shop, in the street, wherever he was. All that he had not been with her when naked he would try to be with someone new. New and young. But false. False to his abandoned talents. False to the best in him that would be for ever lost now, for ever lost. How strange that he should have left it all so soon, so young, so long ago. How strange that all these years he had been busy with maps, with paper ghosts of finding, with finding-masturbation, and all the finding in him dead! There was nothing left for him to do but die now, really. Poor fool, poor mad failed son and husband. She took her wedding ring out of the drawer, threw it on the floor, stamped it out of shape, put it back in the drawer.

Jachin-Boaz's wife no longer cared where Jachin-Boaz was, but she felt a strong need to write a letter to him. She reasoned that he would certainly be working at a map shop or a book and map shop wherever he might be. From the information-gatherers who worked on the special-order maps she obtained the names and addresses of the principal journals of the book trade in five foreign capitals. In each of the journals she placed an advertisement notifying Jachin-Boaz that there was a letter for him to be had at the box number given. To each journal she sent a copy of her letter to him:

Jachin-Boaz,

What are you looking for with your master map that you stole from your son, with your savings that you stole from your wife and child? What will your map show you? Where is your lion? You can find nothing now. For you there never were, never could be lions, failed man. Once you had talent, power of mind and clarity of thought, but they are gone. You have taken yourself away from all order, you have hurled yourself into chaos. What was fresh and sweet in you has gone stale and sour. You are the garbage of yourself.

You will wake up one morning and realize, whoever is beside you, what you have thrown away, what you have done. You have destroyed me as a woman and you have destroyed yourself, your life. You have been committing slow suicide ever since you failed your examinations, and soon you will come to the end of it.

Your father with his cigars, his theatrics, his mistress that you never knew about until I told you – your father, the great man, died at fifty-two. His heart was bad, and he died of it. You are now forty-seven, and you too have a bad heart.

You will wake in the night—whoever lies with you cannot hold back death—and you will hear the beating of your heart that moves always towards the last beat, the last moment. Wherever you are, whomever you are with; you have only a few years left to you, and suddenly they will all be gone. The last moment will be *now*, and you will know what you have lost, and that despairing thought will be your last.

You will want to come back to me, but you cannot come back. You can go only one way now—to the end you have chosen.

These are the last words you will ever have from
the woman who was
once your wife.

When Jachin-Boaz's wife had posted off the five copies of the letter she felt fresh and clear and clean. As she walked back from the post office (she could have trusted no one else with that errand, had felt that she must see with her own eyes the letters disappear into the slot) it seemed to her that she saw the sky, felt the sunlight and the air on her face for the first time in months. A burst of pigeons upward from the square was like the winging up of her spirit in her. Her step was youthful, her eyes bright. A man younger than she turned to look at her in the street. She smiled, he smiled back. I will live long, she thought. I have strong life in me.

At the shop she hummed songs that she had not remembered for years. An old man came in, stains on his clothes, flecks of tobacco and dandruff. *He* won't live to be as old as this one, she thought.

'Stroller's map?' the old man said. 'New one out yet?'

'Voyeur's map, you mean?' said Jachin-Boaz's wife with a bright smile.

'I don't speak French,' said the old man, and winked.

She went to a cabinet, opened a file drawer, took out cards. 'Two alleys crossed off,' she said. 'The servant girl at the bedroom window has gone, and the new one draws the curtains. The house where the two girls always kept the lights on is up for sale and empty now. The revised map isn't ready yet.'

The old man nodded as if it were nothing to him one way or the other, and pretended to be interested in paperbacks.

'Let me show you a pasture map,' said Jachin-Boaz's wife. 'You can watch sheep and cows. You've no idea what goes on at farms.' She was laughing. The old man became red in the face, turned and left the shop, stumbling against the lion door-stop at the open door. Through the shop window Jachin-Boaz's wife watched him going down the street. Dogs trotted past without looking at him.

Later that day the surveyor who had told Boaz-Jachin what he knew about maps came in. He was tall, with a weathered face and an aura of distance, desert wind in open spaces. He gave Jachin-Boaz's wife the special-order maps he had been working on.

'Some people', he said when they had finished their business, 'don't need maps. They make places for themselves, and they always know where they are. To me you seem such a person.'

'I don't need maps,' said Jachin-Boaz's wife. 'Maps are nothing to me. A map pretends to show you what's there, but that's a lie. Nothing's there unless you make it be there.'

'Ah,' said the surveyor. 'But how many people know that? That you can't learn—either you know it or you don't.'

'I know it,' she said.

'Ah,' said the surveyor. 'You! I'll tell you something—

with a woman like you my whole life might have been different.'

'You talk as if your whole life's behind you,' she said. 'You're not that old.' She leaned forward over the counter. He leaned towards her. Music drifted down from the coffee shop upstairs. The assistant rang up a sale and rattled money in the till. The lion at the door seemed to smile as customers came in, went out. She kept the door open most of the time now. 'A man like you', said Jachin-Boaz's wife, 'could be of great value to oil companies, foreign investors. A monthly newsletter, for instance, with the latest information on property and development trends. Who knows what you might do if you cared to? A man who knows what's what, who sees what can be done and puts his hand to it ... ' She saw bright offices, large windows overlooking the sea, charts on the walls, teletypes clicking, conferences, telephones with many pushbuttons, international visitors, articles in business magazines. She picked up the maps he had brought in, laid them down again. 'Boundaries,' she said. 'Wells. Water wells. Did you ever hear of a water millionaire? How are water shares doing on the stock exchange?' They both laughed.

'You see what I mean?' said the surveyor. 'I think little thoughts, you think big ones. Ah!' They leaned towards each other across the counter, both humming the tune that was drifting down from the coffee shop. 'Perhaps we could have dinner this evening?' he said.

'I'd like that,' said Jachin-Boaz's wife. That afternoon she left the assistant to close the shop, and went upstairs early. She lay in the bathtub for a long time, steeping in the silky heat of the steaming water, smelling the scented bubbles, feeling back to the youth still somewhere in her, the excitement of an evening out. She remembered painting quiet landscapes when she was at university, afternoons of sunshine and her hair blowing in the wind. She would get her paintbox out of the cupboard. She would paint again, sit in quiet places in the sun, feel the wind. Green places.

She dressed, made up her face carefully, practised relaxing her mouth in front of the steamy mirror. In the twilight she went up to the roof, looked at the palms in the square darkening in the fading light. She remembered a song that her father used to sing, sang it softly to herself while the evening breeze stirred her hair:

> Where the morning sees the shadows
> Of the orange grove, there was nothing twenty
>     years ago.
> Where the dry wind sowed the desert
> We brought water, planted seedlings, now the
>     oranges grow.

She had bent her wedding ring back into a circle and put it on, and she touched it now. She remembered Boaz-Jachin as a baby laughing in his bath in the sink, remembered herself singing in the kitchen and Jachin-Boaz young. She shut the memories out of her mind. She thought of the five copies of the letter she had posted, and smiled. Pigeons circled the square, and she cried.

# 20

A mighty fortress is our God, sang Gretel in her mind, hearing the voices of the choir in the church of the town where she had been born as she stood behind the counter in the bookshop. Painted on the wooden gallery-front were Bible pictures, pink faces, blue and scarlet robes, too much colour, leaving a taste of marzipan in the eye. The three crosses on Golgotha, black sky, grey clouds. The Resurrection with many golden beams of light, Jesus in white goose-flesh. Potiphar's wife, lusty, opulent, clutching at Joseph.

From deep despair I cry to thee, sang the choir in her mind. The dead nobles in the crypt beneath the altar were only acoustics now. Sound-absorbers, however gauntleted and sworded, fierce in battle and the chase, dead wives virtuous beside them. Silent they were below the altar, but clamorous in stone monuments in the sanctuary, praying in stone effigy, noisy with stone silence in the hymn. From deep despair I cry to thee, Lord God hear thou my call. The street outside the shop moved slowly in its daily march of buses, cars, pedestrians. 'Do you sell ball-point pens?' a lady asked.

'No,' said Gretel. 'Try the newsagent at the corner.'

'Greeting cards?'

'No,' said Gretel. 'Sorry, books only.' Apple cores came into her mind. Why apple cores, what apple cores? Brown apple cores in the autumn in a neighbour's garden. Yellow leaves and she scuffling among them, squatting to eat the apple cores dropped there by someone else. Baskets of apples at home. Why had she wanted someone else's brown cores? How old had she been? Five, perhaps, or six. Her earliest memory. What did Jachin-Boaz dream of? What waited for him in his sleep? What waited for him outside in the early morning? How could he go out into the street and come back with claw-marks on his arm? What was the meat for? Something that he was afraid of. Something that could kill him. Something that he wanted to be killed by? A man could not be completely a liar in his lovemaking. Jachin-Boaz made love like a man who wanted to live, a man who wanted her. How could he be so full of life and so full of despair? His face above her in bed was easy and loving, the morning face before the dawn was haggard, haunted.

'Perhaps we could have lunch one day soon?' That was what he had said to her that first time, after buying a book on string quartets. She had had another man at that time. Wednesdays and weekends. It isn't that I don't want to marry you, he said. It would kill my mother if I married a girl who wasn't Jewish. Right. Here's another one. Perhaps we could have lunch one day soon. Yes, let's have lunch. My people killed six million of you. He had brought her a single rose. A yellow one that day, red ones later. She had talked about her dead father. No one else had asked about her father, invited him from the silence. He had kissed her hand when he said goodbye outside the shop. This was not, she had felt, going to be Wednesdays and weekends. She wanted to belong wholly to a man, and this man's quiet face was claiming her and she was afraid.

Now his haunted face awoke beside her every morning. A mighty fortress, sang Gretel in her mind, imposing her will on the choir. The sound surged into a lion-coloured roar, a strong river of violent ... what? Not joy. Life. Violent life. I knew that I'd be happy with him, unhappy with him — everything, and more of everything than ever before in my life. Something there is that won't die. A mighty fortress is our something.

# 2I

The night sky, pinky-grey, leaned close to chimneys, rooftops, hesitantly touched black bridges and the winding river. I am beautiful only if you look at me, the sky said.

I can't be everybody, said Jachin-Boaz, wise with the mind of sleep and knowing his dream for a dream. His words were an answer to which the question was a sensation of something very big, something very small. Which part of it am I?

Ha ha, laughed the answer, strutting in the mind that would forget it on awakening. See how simple it is? Male or female? Choose.

Something very big, something very small, thought Jachin-Boaz. There is a sob I don't let out, there is a curse I don't speak, there is a turning away from whom, there is a black shoulder of what?

Well, said the answer, this is the place you tried to avoid, but it is not to be avoided.

I can cover it with a map, said Jachin-Boaz. Then there will be world.

He spread out the map, so thin! Like tissue paper. The black shoulder heaved up through it, tore it. As from a heaving mountain Jachin-Boaz fell away.

I can cover it with a map, he said again, spreading vast miles-wide tissue paper over the black abyss. He ran lightly across its surface that billowed in a dreadful rising black wind. See! he cried as he fell through the tearing tissue paper, I'm not falling!

Right, said the answer. See how simple? Betrayed or

betrayer? Choose. Either way you win the loss of every-thing.

I cry in the throat, said Jachin-Boaz.

Yes, said the answer.

I curse in the dark, said Jachin-Boaz.

Yes, said the answer.

From me all turns away, said Jachin-Boaz.

Loss unending, said the answer.

She will save, said Jachin-Boaz.

Whom you betray, the answer said.

He will save, said Jachin-Boaz.

Who turns away, the answer said.

World is there if I hold fast to it, said Jachin-Boaz.

What is there if you let go? the answer said. Dare to find out?

I'll let go if I can hold on while I'm doing it, said Jachin-Boaz. Lion-skins make stronger maps than tissue paper, he thought. He stood on the window ledge looking down. Far below him the firemen held taut the lion-skin.

No use telling me to jump, said Jachin-Boaz. Not even in a dream.

We all know what a no is shaped like, said the answer.

Right, said Jachin-Boaz. We know and the noes know.

Had your noes cut off lately? said the answer.

Come closer, said Jachin-Boaz darkly to the answer. It was very big, and he was very small and frightened. He woke up with his heart beating fast, remembering nothing.

Half-past four, said the clock on the night table. The lion would be waiting. Let him starve, thought Jachin-Boaz, and went back to sleep.

# 22

'I can't find it,' said Boaz-Jachin in his own language, talking in his sleep.

'What?' said the girl beside him in the narrow upper berth in the pre-dawn dimness of the stateroom. She spoke English.

'Where to go,' said Boaz-Jachin, still asleep, still speaking in his own language.

'What are you saying?' said the girl.

'Ugly maps. Can't make nice maps. Only where I've been,' said Boaz-Jachin. 'Lost,' he said in English as he woke up.

'What's lost? Are you lost?'

'What time is it?' said Boaz-Jachin. 'I have to get back to the crew's quarters before breakfast.' He looked at his wristwatch. Half-past four.

'Are you always lost?' said the girl. They were nested like two spoons, her nakedness warm and insistent against his back, her mouth close to his ear. Through the porthole the darkness was greying. Boaz-Jachin tried to remember his dream.

'Are you always lost?' said the girl.

Boaz-Jachin wished that she would be quiet, tried to call back the vanished dream. 'Everything that is found is always lost again,' he said.

'Yes,' said the girl. 'That's good. That's true. Is it yours or did you read it?'

'Hush,' said Boaz-Jachin, trying to fit into a silence with her. The porthole was like a blind eye in the dim stateroom.

On that round blind eye, whitening with the morning fog behind it, he seemed to see his map, the one he had newly drawn from memory after he and the trader had been picked up by the big white cruise ship: his town, his house, Lila's house, the bus depot and the other bus depot, the road to the citadel, the hall of the lion-hunt reliefs, the hill where he had sat, the road to the seaport, the place where the lorry driver had dropped him, the brief distance with the woman in the red car, the farm where the dying father had written FORGIVE with his finger, the *Swallow*'s track to Rising Son Rocks. The city where he thought his father was now with the other better map, the map of his future.

The map faded, only the round blind stare of the fog was left. In that stare Boaz-Jachin doubted that his father's map would be of any use to him. He had remembered it as large and beautiful. Now he thought of it as small and cramped, too neat, too calculated, too little cognizant of unknown places, of the night places waiting beyond the day places, of the somewheres dropping from the open wombs of nowheres. He felt lost as he had not done since being with the lion.

'Maps,' he said softly. 'A map is the dead body of where you've been. A map is the unborn baby of where you're going. There are no maps. Maps are pictures of what isn't. I don't want it.'

'That's beautiful,' said the girl. ' "There are no maps." What don't you want?'

'My father's map,' said Boaz-Jachin.

'That's good,' said the girl. 'Is it yours? Do you write? It sounds like the beginning of a poem: "My father's map is ... " What is it?'

'His,' said Boaz-Jachin. 'And he can keep it.' He threw back the sheets, rolled the girl over on her stomach, bit her buttocks, got out of bed and put his clothes on.

'I'll show you my poems tonight,' she said.

'All right,' said Boaz-Jachin, as the girl's room-mate, yawning, came back from where she had spent the night. He went back to the crew's quarters and got ready to serve breakfast to the first sitting.

The trader had been dropped off at the last port. Boaz-Jachin, signed on to replace a waiter who had left earlier in the cruise, would stay with the ship until it reached its home port. From there he could travel overland most of the way to the city where he expected to find his father. Boaz-Jachin no longer wanted the map, but he wanted to find his father and tell him so. While serving breakfast that morning he thought about what he would say to his father.

Keep it, he would say. I don't need it. I don't need maps. At first he imagined himself only, saw and heard himself saying the words without seeing his father in his mind. Then he tried to imagine Jachin-Boaz. Perhaps he would be lying in a dirty bed, unshaven, ill, maybe dying. Or dim and pale, lost in some shop of dust and shadows in the great city, or standing alone on a bridge in the rain, looking down at the water, defeated. What have you found with your map? he would say to Jachin-Boaz his father. Has the future you drew so beautifully for me come to you? Has it made you happy?

The dishes clattered, the music played anonymously its tunes that were the same in airports, cocktail bars and lifts, the children quarrelled and left their eggs uneaten. The parents sat with the faces and necks of every day coming out of their holiday clothes, spongy backs and flabby arms of women in sun-back dresses, festive trousers on men with office feet. Girls displayed in the shops of their summer dresses the stock that had not moved all year, their mouths open with surrender, their eyes blurred with hope or sharp with arithmetic.

Boaz-Jachin walked behind his smile, served from behind his eyes, looked down on bald heads, bosoms, brushed ardent shoulders with his thighs, said thank you, nodded, smiled, cleared away, walked back and forth through swinging doors and galley smells. Every person here had had a father and a mother. Every person here had been a child. The thought was staggering. The feet of the men in the festive trousers made him want to cry.

Boaz-Jachin served the table of the girl he had slept with last night. She shaped the word *hello* with her mouth, touched his leg with her hand. He looked down her dress at her breasts, thought of last night and the night that was coming. He looked up and saw her father looking at him.

The father's face was busy with horn-rimmed glasses and a beard. The father's eyes were sad. The father's eyes spoke suddenly to Boaz-Jachin. You can and I can't, said the father's eyes.

Boaz-Jachin looked at the mother looking at the father. Her face was saying something that his mother's face had often said. But he had never paid attention to what it was. Forget this, remember that, said her face. What was the *this* to be forgotten? What was the *that* to be remembered? Boaz-Jachin thought of the road to the port and of the time after the lorry driver when it seemed to him that he could speak with animals, trees, stones.

Beyond the windows of the dining room the sea sparkled in the sunlight. Part of an island passed, a straggle of ruins, a broken citadel, the pillars of a temple, two figures on a hill. Gulls rose and fell on the air currents beside the ship. This, said the sea. Only this. What? thought Boaz-Jachin. Who? Who is looking out through the eyeholes in my face? No one, said the sea. Only this.

'Thank you,' said Boaz-Jachin serving the mother, averting his eyes from her bosom.

That night again he went to the girl's stateroom.

'Wait,' she said as he began to take his clothes off. 'I want to read you some poems.'

'I just want to be comfortable,' said Boaz-Jachin. 'I can listen with my clothes off.'

'All right,' she said. She took a thick folder from a drawer. The sea and the sky outside were dark, the ship thrust cleaving its phosphorescent bow wave, the engines hummed, the air-conditioning whirred, the lamp by the berth made a cosy glow. 'They mostly don't have titles,' she said, and began to read:

> Black rock rising to a neverness of sky,
> Black alone, no sky above the
> Far-down lost and winding
> Blood-red river and my
> Frail black boat, dead
> God my freight, too heavy for my
> Craft, blind broken eyes.
> Blind father-stone between my thighs ...

'Shit,' said Boaz-Jachin. 'Another father.'

> ... Deflower my death, seed
> My defeat, get NOW from nothing,
> Fierce upon your daughter.
> Lot was made drunk, salt
> Wife behind him in the
> Desert. Stone is my lot, dead
> God my steersman.
> Blind,
> Find
> Star.

'What do you think?' said the girl when she had finished reading.

124

'I don't want to think,' said Boaz-Jachin. 'Can't we not-think for a while?' He pulled her T-shirt over her head, kissed her breasts. She twisted away from him.

'Is that all I am?' she said. 'Something to grab, something to fuck?'

Boaz-Jachin bit her flank hopefully but with lessening conviction. She sat motionless, looking thoughtful.

'You're beautiful,' she said, ruffling his hair. 'Am I beautiful to you?'

'Yes,' said Boaz-Jachin, unbuttoning her jeans. She rolled away with her jeans still on.

'No, I'm not,' she said. She lay on her stomach, leafing through the poems in the folder. 'You're saying I am because you want to fuck. Not even make love, just fuck. I'm not beautiful to you.'

'All right,' said Boaz-Jachin. 'You're not beautiful to me.' He sat up, got off the bed, put on his trousers.

'Come back,' she said. 'You don't mean that either.'

Boaz-Jachin took off his trousers, climbed back into the berth. When they were both naked he looked down at her face. 'Now you're beautiful,' he said.

'Shit,' she said, and turned away. She lay with her face averted, inert while Boaz-Jachin tried to make love. 'Oh,' she whimpered.

'What's the matter?'

'You're hurting me.'

Boaz-Jachin lost his erection, withdrew. 'The hell with it,' he said.

'Daughters are supposed to attract their fathers sexually,' said the girl as he lay beside her, sulking, 'but I don't. I'm not beautiful to him either. He once told me that boys would love me for my mind. In some ways he's rotten.'

'My God!' said Boaz-Jachin. 'I am so sick and tired of

fathers!' He sat up, swung his legs over the edge of the berth.

'Don't go away,' she said. 'Goddam it, have I got to plead for every lousy minute of human companionship? Have I got to pay for every minute of attention with my pussy? Can't you talk to me, just one person to another? Can't you give anything but your prick? And even that isn't given — you're only taking.'

Boaz-Jachin felt his childhood vanish as if he had been launched from it in a rocket. As if with ancient knowledge he recognized the departure of innocence and simplicity from his life. He groaned, and lay back on the pillow staring at the ceiling. Lila seemed long ago, never to be found again.

'What do you want me to do?' he said.

'Talk to me. *Be* with me. Be with *me*, not just parts of me.'

'Oh God,' said Boaz-Jachin. She was right. He was wrong. He hadn't wanted to be with *her*. He had sensed that she would be willing and he wanted a girl to cuddle with, a no one. But everybody was a someone. He cursed his new knowledge. He had known this girl for a few days only, and it seemed a lifetime of mistakes. He felt roped together with her on the sheer face of a bleak mountain. He felt immensely weary.

'What?' she said, looking at his face. 'What's the matter?'

Boaz-Jachin stared at the ceiling, remembering Lila and the first night on the roof, remembering the brightness of the stars and how it was to feel good and know nothing. The lion came into his mind and was gone, leaving emptiness that urged him forward.

'What do you want to do?' the girl said. 'I don't mean now, this minute. In life, I mean.'

What *do* I want to do? thought Boaz-Jachin. I want to find my father so I can tell him I don't want his map. That's not a lifetime career. 'Shit,' he said.

'You're a real intellectual,' said the girl. 'You're a real deep thinker. Try to say something in words, just for the novelty of it.'

'I don't know what I want to do,' said Boaz-Jachin.

'You're a very interesting person,' said the girl. 'I don't meet people as interesting as you every day in the week. Tell me more about yourself. Now that we've been to bed, let's get acquainted. Have you ever done anything? Have you ever written a poem, for instance, or painted a picture? Do you play a musical instrument? I'm trying to remember why I *did* go to bed with you. You were beautiful and you said something good. You said that you were looking for your father who was looking for a lion, and I said there were no lions any more, and you said there was one lion and one wheel, and I said that was beautiful, and then all you wanted to do was fuck.'

Boaz-Jachin was out of the berth and putting his clothes on. 'I play the guitar,' he said. 'I drew an ugly map that I lost, and then I drew another map. I copied a photograph of a lion once. I've never written a poem. I've never painted a picture.' He was angry, but as he spoke he became unaccountably elated, proud. There was something in him not drained off by poems or pictures, something unknown, unavailable but undiminished, intact, waiting to be found. He tried to find it, found only emptiness, was ashamed then, humbled, felt mistaken in his temporary pride, shook his head, opened the door and stepped out into the corridor.

As he closed the stateroom door behind him he saw the girl's father coming towards him. The father's face became very red. He stopped before Boaz-Jachin, his face working behind the horn-rimmed glasses and the beard.

'Good evening, sir,' said Boaz-Jachin, although it was the middle of the night. He attempted to walk around the father, but the father stepped in front of him, blocking his way. He was a small man, no taller than Boaz-Jachin, but Boaz-Jachin felt in the wrong and looked it.

' "Good evening, sir!" ' mimicked the father with a dreadful grimace. 'Good evening, father number such-and-such of girl number such-and-such. Just like that. Smooth and easy.'

Boaz-Jachin saw in his mind a map of the sea, its islands and ports. If he were put off at the next port because of a passenger complaint he would have another sea voyage to make, another boat or ship to find, other people with their lives and histories to drag him down with hard and heavy knowledge. It was as if his shirt and all his pockets were filled with great lumpy potatoes of unwanted knowledge. He wished that he could be at the end of his journey and not have to talk to anyone for a while.

'Excuse me, please, sir,' he said. Still the father blocked his way.

'What are you?' said the father. 'For you life must be one girl after another, and sometimes an older woman who pays you a little something for your services, I suppose. Now you're a waiter on a cruise ship, now a beach boy at a resort. You get the daughters that fathers have stayed up with when they were sick, have listened to the troubles of, have wanted the best for. You with your smooth face and clear eyes and long hair.'

Boaz-Jachin sat down on the floor, his arms resting on his drawn-up knees. He shook his head. He was almost on the point of crying, but he began to laugh.

'And that's funny to you?' said the father.

'You don't know what I'm laughing at,' said Boaz-Jachin. 'Nothing is smooth and easy for me, and my life isn't one girl after another—it seems to be one father after another. And how would it help you if I had a wrinkled face and clouded eyes and short hair? Would your daughter then become a nun?'

The father's face relaxed behind the beard and the glasses. 'It's hard to let go,' he said.

'And it's hard to hold on,' said Boaz-Jachin.

'To what?' said the father.

'The wheel,' said Boaz-Jachin.

'Ah,' said the father. 'I know that wheel.' He smiled and sat down beside Boaz-Jachin. They sat together on the floor, smiling while the ship hummed, the air-conditioning whirred, and the dark sea slipped by on either side.

# 23

Darkness roared with the lion, the night stalked with the silence of him. The lion was. Ignorant of non-existence he existed. Ignorant of self he was a sunlit violence with calm joy at the centre of it, he was the violence of being-as-hunter constantly renewed in the devouring of non-being. The wheel had been when he ran tawny on the plain, printing his motion on the grateful air. He had died biting the wheel that went on and left him dead. The wheel continued, the lion continued. He was intact, diminished by nothing, increased by nothing, absolute. He ate meat or he did not eat meat, was seen or unseen, known when there was knowledge of him, unknown when there was not. But always he was.

For him there were no maps, no places, no time. Beneath his tread the round earth rolled, the wheel turned, bearing him to death and life again. Through his lion-being drifted stars and blackness, morning sang, night soothed, dawn burst its daylight from the womb of vital terror. Oceans heaved, frail bridges spanned the winding track of days, the rising air sang lion-flight in wings of birds. In clocks ticked lion-time. It pulsed in heartbeats, footsteps walking all unknowing, souls of guilt and sorrow, souls of love and pain. He had been called, he had come. He was.

# 24

After his last encounter with the lion Jachin-Boaz felt childish, stupid, shaken. That the lion had turned his back on him now frightened him more than the previous attack. He felt as if the present had vomited him out like a Jonah. He lay gasping on dry land under the eye of an exacting God. 'There is no God,' he said, 'but the exactions exist, so there might just as well be a God. Perhaps there is one after all.'

'People always assume that God is with people,' said Gretel. 'But maybe God is in the furniture, or with stones.'

Go and preach, thought Jachin-Boaz, his mind still on Jonah. The king sleeps with his chariots, the lions are dead. I have not marked the lion-palace on my master-map. Boaz-Jachin's master-map. I have a lion, and I have told him about a cowboy suit.

He tried to remember why his old life had seemed intolerable. Admittedly he had not felt himself to be a whole man, but at least he had been a reasonably comfortable failed man, lacking nothing but his testicles. If only he could have the comfort of his mife, his wife rather, without his wife! Whother, whether he could get along without her he doubted. Despite his new-found maleness it seemed that he had nothing, was nothing. He marvelled that he went on making love with Gretel. Something in me lives its own life, full of appetite, he thought. Where am I while this is going on? On what map?

Why am I afraid now? he thought. When I was impotent I was secure. It isn't safe to have balls. Now I ramp like a stallion while my soul is sick with terror. Stallions surely aren't afraid, lions aren't afraid. I have a lion. I don't have a lion—a lion has me. A lion hallucinates me. To a lion appears Jachin-Boaz in the early morning. When I was impotent I was safe. What was all that nonsense about wanting my manhood, idiot that I am? Let him starve, that lion. I don't want to see him. They can go on transmitting but I won't receive.

For several days Jachin-Boaz, awaking at the usual time, went back to sleep, sulking, while in his imagination the lion grew thinner daily. Beside him every morning at half-past four Gretel woke up, waiting with closed eyes for him to go out while Jachin-Boaz went back to sleep, dreaming dreams he would not remember.

Jachin-Boaz was dreaming. With a microscope he was looking at an illuminated drop of water. In the water swam a green and spherical form of many-celled animal-algae. Thousands of tiny moving whips on its surface made it revolve its green-jewelled globe like a little world.

Jachin-Boaz increased the magnification, looked deep into one of the hundreds of cells. Closer, closer through the luminous green. Oh yes, he said. The naked figures of his father and mother copulated in the brilliant field of the lens with darkness all around them. So big and he so small. A shoulder turning away within the luminous green world in the drop of water.

The cell withdrew, grew small, receded into the green and turning world that closed up again, its whips propelling it in sparkling revolutions.

*Unlike the infinitely ongoing asexual amoeba,* said the lecturer, *this organism has differentiated within itself male and female cells. Sexual reproduction occurs, followed by another phenomenon unknown to the amoeba: death. In the words of one naturalist, 'It must die because it has had children and is no longer needed.' That is why this wheel dies. The invention of the wheel is nothing compared to the invention of death, and this wheel invented death.*

Jachin-Boaz increased the magnification again, again looked into the same cell. Darkness in the brilliance. His mother cried out. The lecturer, nodding in a chalk-dusted grey suit, came between him and what was happening in the darkness. *This is the wheel that invented death,* he said.

Jachin-Boaz hurled himself into the dark and shining tube of the microscope, saw the green wheel bright before him, leaped upon it, holding it to him, trying to stop its turning.

The wheel won't die, he said, biting it, tasting its wet greenness. This wheel has had children but he doesn't die. The lions die.

*It seems a kind of intellectual suicide,* said the lecturer, looking down on Jachin-Boaz who lay in a paper coffin, his beard aimed up at the lecturer whose beard was aiming down at him.

Now you're dead, said Jachin-Boaz to the lecturer. But the paper coffin lid came down on Jachin-Boaz. No, he said. You, not me. Turn it around. Let the little green cells die instead. It's always I who die. It was I then and it's I now. When is it my turn, when the others die?

*It keeps turning but it's not your turn,* said the lecturer. *Never your turn.*

My turn, said Jachin-Boaz. He was walking away from the coffin, looking back at it and noticing that it was much shorter than before. There was no father's beard sticking up. The hand that held the map was smaller, younger. My turn, my turn, he wept, smelled the lion, wept and whimpered in his sleep.

Gretel woke up, leaned on her elbow, looked at Jachin-Boaz in the dim light, looked at his bandaged arm that he flung over his face. She looked at her watch. Four o'clock. She turned on her side away from Jachin-Boaz and lay there, awake.

At half-past four Jachin-Boaz awoke, feeling tired. He did not remember his dream. He bathed, shaved, dressed, took meat for the lion, and went out.

The lion was standing across the street. Jachin-Boaz crossed to him, threw him the meat, watched him eat. With the lion-smell in his nostrils he turned and walked towards the embankment, not looking back.

When Jachin-Boaz and the lion had gone some distance down the street towards the river a police constable stepped out from behind a corner of the building where Jachin-Boaz lived. He stepped back as Gretel came out, fully dressed, with a carrier-bag in one hand.

Gretel looked towards the river, then followed Jachin-Boaz and the lion.

The police constable waited a few moments, then followed Gretel.

Jachin-Boaz walked along the embankment on the side away from the river. He stopped at a garden above which rose a statue of a man who had been beheaded after a theological dispute with a king. There was a bench on the pavement. Near it was a telephone kiosk. The sky was cloudy, the before-dawn light was grey, the bridges were black over the quiet river.

Jachin-Boaz turned and faced the lion. Down the street a girl with a carrier-bag stepped into a doorway. Beyond her a man's dark figure turned into a side street. There was no one else in sight.

Jachin-Boaz sat down on the bench. The lion lay down on the pavement five yards away, his eyes on Jachin-Boaz's face.

'Always the frown, like my father,' said Jachin-Boaz. 'How was I to be a scientist, father Lion? Science is knowing. What could I have known? Others always did the knowing, knew what was in me, what should come out of me, what was best for me. I didn't know who I was, what I wanted. I know less now, and I am afraid.'

The sound of his own voice and the words he was saying became boring to Jachin-Boaz. He felt a wave of irritation flooding through him. He didn't want to say what he was saying. What did the lion want? The lion was real, could kill him, might very well do it at any moment. Jachin-Boaz felt himself disappearing into terror, felt himself coming back, went on.

'My thoughts are useless to me, and I cannot remember my dreams. I have forgotten more of my life than I remember, and with my forgetting I have lost my being. You expect something of me, father Lion. Maybe only my death. Maybe you are too late for that. Maybe I have beaten you to it. Not that my death belongs to me.

'One of my teachers said it was an intellectual suicide when I failed my examinations. But science is knowing, and how could I know anything, how make a profession of knowing? Little things, yes. Places on a map.

'When you kill yourself you kill the world, but it doesn't die. He'd had a bad heart for some time, so it couldn't have been my fault altogether. Why did he never talk to *me*? Why did he seem always to be talking to a space that I hadn't moved into? Why was he always holding up an empty suit of clothes for me to jump into? He talked to clothes I never did put on. A sleeve with no arm in it struck him down. An empty shoulder turned away from him. He closed his mouth and lay down, but he is more alive in me than I am.

'I am a coward, and you are patient with me. You are a sporting lion. You want my death to stand up like a man in me before you spring. You have contempt for anything that turns away.

'But if you kill me I shall then be more alive than ever,

strong as the brazen tyre on the wheel. My son will feel me heavy and unfinished on his back, big in his mind.'

Jachin-Boaz was silent for a time, then stood up. 'Perhaps I too have never spoken to my son,' he said, 'but to an empty place where he was not. Now I talk to you, his anger. I will stand before you, look at you. If I did not look at him at least I will look at you, his rage. My rage. Can I roar like you? Can I make a big sound of whole anger?' Jachin-Boaz tried to roar, broke off in coughing.

The lion crouched, gathering himself, lashing his tail. The lion roared, and the river of lion-sound rolled beside the other river, thunderous under the broken sky.

'No!' cried Gretel, running towards the lion from behind. 'No!' She had thrown away the carrier-bag, and held the carving knife she had concealed in it. She held the knife in the manner of knife-fighters, with the blade extending the line of her wrist, ready to thrust in and up.

'Get back!' shouted Jachin-Boaz. But the lion had turned at the sound of Gretel's voice. Jachin-Boaz saw the muscles bunching for the leap, threw himself on the lion's back as it sprang, his fingers locked in its mane, his face buried in the coarse rank hair.

The lion, turning his head to seize Jachin-Boaz's right arm in his jaws, landed short as Gretel jumped aside.

'Here!' shouted the constable, striking the pavement with his truncheon. 'This won't do! Stop it at once!'

'Into the telephone box!' yelled Jachin-Boaz to the constable. 'Get her into the telephone box!'

But Gretel flung herself at the lion, drove her knife at his throat. The blade was partly deflected by the thick mane, but it went in, and the lion let go of Jachin-Boaz's arm and swung his head around towards Gretel.

'Here!' shouted the constable. He pulled Jachin-Boaz from the lion and thrust Gretel back.

Jachin-Boaz, strong as a madman, hurled himself with arms flung wide at Gretel and the constable, slamming them against the telephone kiosk. Gretel and he together shoved the constable out of the way for long enough to open the door, then pulled him savagely inside.

'No, you don't,' said the constable, his face red. He had been in family situations many times before, and more than once had had the combatants turn on him like this. Simultaneously he gripped the wrist of Gretel's knife hand and brought his knee up into Jachin-Boaz's groin.

'Imbecile!' gasped Jachin-Boaz, sinking to the floor with the pain. In a red and golden haze with black and shooting lights he felt a rage too big for his body, too strong for his voice, immense, unlimited by time, amber-eyed and taloned.

'Good God!' said the constable, staring through the glass door. 'There's a lion out there!'

'Aha!' said Jachin-Boaz, exulting. 'You can see him now! How do you like him! He's big, he's angry. He can say no to anybody, eh?'

The constable, jammed between Gretel and the side of the telephone box, was writhing desperately while Gretel, bloody knife in hand, glared at him wildly. 'I beg your pardon, madame,' he said. 'I am trying to get to the telephone.' He looked away from the lion, dialled his station number, looked back again.

The constable identified himself, reported his location. 'What I think we need here', he said, 'is the fire brigade with a pumper. Big net too. Stout one. No. Not a fire. Animal situation, actually. Yes, I should say so. With a strong cage, you know, as fast as they can. Ambulance too. Well, let's say a large carnivore. No, I'm not. All right, a tiger, if you like. How should I know? Yes, I'll be here. Goodbye.'

As the constable rang off there was a screech of brakes, followed by a crash. Looking past Jachin-Boaz the constable saw two cars stopped on the road, the front of one and the rear of the other crumpled together. Both drivers remained in their cars. Jachin-Boaz and Gretel were looking beyond the cars at the pavement and the parapet along the river.

'Where is it then?' said the constable.

'Where is what?' said Jachin-Boaz.

'The lion,' said the constable.

'Lions are extinct,' said Jachin-Boaz.

'Don't try that on with me, mate,' said the constable. 'Look at your bleeding arm.'

'Spiked fence,' said Jachin-Boaz. 'Stumbled. Fell. Drunk again.'

'What about you, madame?' said the constable.

'I walk in my sleep,' said Gretel. 'I don't know how I got here. This is very embarrassing for me.'

'You two stay here,' said the constable. He opened the door of the telephone kiosk, looked all around, and stepped out. The motorists were still there, sitting in their cars with their windows rolled up. The constable went to the first car, motioned to the driver to lower the window.

'Why'd you stop?' said the constable.

'Quite extraordinary,' said the driver. 'Somehow my foot slipped off the accelerator and came down on the brake. I don't know how it happened.'

'What did you see in front of you when you stopped?' said the constable.

'Nothing at all,' said the driver.

The constable walked back to the second car. 'What did you see?' he said.

'I saw the car in front of me stop so suddenly that I hadn't time to stop myself,' said the driver.

'Nothing else?' said the constable.

'No, indeed,' said the driver.

The constable took the names, addresses and registration numbers of both drivers, and they drove slowly away.

A polyphonic blaring was heard as a fire brigade pumper, an ambulance, a fire brigade car and a police car, all with flashing lights, arrived at high speed and slammed on their brakes. Armed men came out of the police car.

'Where's the tiger?' said the firemen and the police together.

'What tiger?' said the constable.

'I take a dim view of practical jokers, Phillips,' said the police superintendent. 'You called for a pumper and a stout net and an ambulance and some people from the zoo with a cage. Here they are now,' he said as a van pulled up. 'Now where's this large carnivore or tiger or whatever?'

'That call must have been made by this chap here impersonating me while I was unconscious,' said the constable. 'I was trying to break up a fight between this couple, and in the struggle my head struck the corner of the telephone box with such force that I was rendered totally unconscious for a short time.'

'Did you ring up for all this then, while impersonating a police constable?' the superintendent asked Jachin-Boaz.

'I don't know,' said Jachin-Boaz. 'I feel confused.' He was feeling faint. He had taken off his jacket and wrapped it around his arm, and it was now thoroughly soaked with blood.

'What happened to his arm?' the superintendent asked the constable.

'Spiked fence,' said Jachin-Boaz.

'She had a knife,' said the constable. 'Best give it me now, madame,' he said.

Gretel gave him the knife. There was no longer any blood on it.

'Are you putting them on a charge?' said the superintendent.

'I believe', said the constable, 'that these people are in a
mental state that makes them a danger to themselves and to
others, and I think that we had better have them committed for observation under the Mental Health Act.'

One of the men from the zoo came over to Jachin-Boaz.
He was small and dark, looked from side to side constantly
and seemed to be sniffing the air. 'I don't suppose I could
have a look at this gentleman's arm?' he said.

The police constable unwrapped the bloody jacket from
Jachin-Boaz's arm, peeled away the blood-soaked torn
shirt sleeve.

'Yes, indeed,' said the man from the zoo to Jachin-Boaz.
'Very mental. How did you come by these particular teeth-
marks?'

'Spiked fence,' said Jachin-Boaz.

'Knife,' said the constable. 'Also, she may have bitten him
during the struggle.'

'Regular tigress,' said the zoo man smiling, showing his
teeth, sniffing the air.

It was full morning now. The sky had got as light as it was
going to be that day. The clouds over the river promised
rain, the water ran dark and heavy under the bridges. Cars,
cyclists and pedestrians were active on the embankment.
The pumper, with horn blaring and light flashing, went back
to the fire station. The ambulance, also flashing and blaring,
followed with Jachin-Boaz, Gretel and the constable in it.
The police car followed the ambulance.

The zoo van stayed where it was for a time while the
little dark man walked all around the telephone kiosk, back
and forth before the statue of the man who had lost his head
for some notion of truth, and up and down the pavement
along the embankment. He found nothing.

# 25

The world seemed to be owned by a freemasonry of petrol stations, monster tanks and towers and abstract structures of no human agency or purpose. Wires hummed aloft, giant steel legs stalked motionless on frightened landscapes past haystacks, mute blind barns, wagons rotting by dunghills on tracks to isolation where brown dwellings shrugged up from the earth. We knew it long ago, said huts with grass on the roofs. Hills went up and down, cows grazed on silence, goats stared with eyes like oracle stones. Cryptic names and symbols in strong raw colours flashed signals one to the other across the roofs and haystacks, across the stone and lumber of towns and cities. Flesh and blood spoke ineffectually in little voices of breath, feet hurried, plodded, pedalled. Faces passed on the road asked unanswerable questions. You! exclaimed the faces. Us!

The petrol stations, owning the world, called to their brother monsters. Distant towers flashed lights. The petrol stations kept up their pretence, fuelled cars and lorries, maintained the fiction of roads for humans. Vast pipes slid effortlessly over miles of world. Huge valves regulated flow. Lights flashed at sea. Music played in aeroplanes. Never did the music name the pipes and petrol stations, the great steel stalking that laughed with striding legs. God is with us, said the valves and towers. With us, said the stones. Cars moved on roads.

Boaz-Jachin felt the miles spinning out behind him. Mina's leg was warm against his. Her leg was named Mina like all the rest of her now. Her someoneness had established itself in him since the nights in her stateroom.

Words came to his mind unbidden, unresisted. They were there like a smell that carries memory or like a change in the temperature of the air: the father must live so that the father can die. Boaz-Jachin groaned inwardly. Tiresome reversals somersaulting in his brain. Found and lost, always and never, everything and nothing. Where had these new words come from? What was wanted of him? What had he to do with such things?

No longer subtle as air, but now like sudden men in armour, implacable, cold with the night wind of a road hard ridden, barbarous with savage unknown meaning useless to resist: the father must live so that the father can die. Quickly! What quickly? Hot waves of irritation leaped in Boaz-Jachin like flames. He sweated, ignorant and anxious.

'Petrol stations own the world,' said Mina. 'Tanks and towers signal one to the other in strong raw colours. Goats have eyes like oracle stones.'

'That's very well observed,' said her father. 'They do. Urim and Thummim.'

Stop telling me everything, thought Boaz-Jachin. Stop presenting the world. I'll see the goats and the petrol stations or I won't. Let them be whatever they'll be to me.

'Isn't anybody but me hungry?' said Mina's mother.

'There's a book you have to read,' said Mina to Boaz-Jachin. 'It's a poet's notebook.'

No, I don't have to read it, he thought. Quickly. What quickly? A breathless sense of hurry rose in him like a whirlwind.

'That part about the uncle's death or the grandfather's death, how it was so strong in him and took so long,' said the father. 'Unforgettable.'

'I know,' said Mina. 'And the man who walked funny that he followed in the street.'

'I'm *starving*,' said the mother.

'Take a look at the guide,' said the father. 'Where are we on the map?'

'You know how I am with maps,' said the mother. 'It takes me a long time.' She unfolded the map clumsily.

'Look,' said the father, pointing with his finger on the map. 'We're over here somewhere, heading north.'

'Keep your eyes on the road,' said the mother. 'And I wish you'd stop driving so fast. We passed a place about five miles back that looked good, and it was gone before I could tell you to slow down.'

'There,' said Mina.

'What?' said the father.

'It had an orange tree in a red clay courtyard,' said Mina. 'There were white doves.'

'I can turn round,' said the father.

'Never mind,' said Mina. 'I'm not even sure it was a restaurant.'

'Where are we?' said the father. 'Have you found us on the map yet?'

'You make me so nervous when I have to look at a map that my hands shake,' said the mother.

The rented car hummed to itself. Whatever happens is not my fault, said the car. From ahead the miles surged towards them in numberless sharp-focused grains of road that rolled beneath the wheels and spun out behind. Boaz-Jachin felt stifled in the car with Mina and her parents. He drew deep breaths, expelled them slowly. He wished that he had not accepted their offer of a lift. He wished that he had a guitar again and were travelling alone and more slowly. But he felt compelled to hurry. Emptiness leaped forward in him, rushing towards something.

'*That* road!' said the mother. 'There! About five miles down there's an old inn, five forks and spoons in the guide. We've passed it now. You simply *refuse* to slow down.'

The father swung the car around in a U-turn, sideswiped a van just then overtaking him, slewed off the road, up a bank, and crashed into a tree. Broken headlights tinkled. Steam drifted from the smashed radiator. All was silent for a moment. Not *my* fault, said the car.

It's her fault, thought the father.

It's his fault, thought the mother.

It's both their faults, thought Mina.

It's the kind of thing that can be expected from this family, thought Boaz-Jachin. I'll be lucky if I get away from them with my life.

The petrol stations, the valves and towers, the giant steel legs that strode across the landscape said nothing.

Everyone looked at everyone else. No one seemed injured.

'My God,' said the mother.

'Right,' said the father. 'Very good. We can walk to the goddam famous old five-fork-and-spoon inn.'

'My God,' said the mother. 'My neck.'

'What's the matter with your neck?' said the father.

'I don't know,' said the mother. 'It feels all right now, but sometimes you don't get the full effects of backlash until months later.'

'But it feels all right now,' said the father.

'I don't know,' said the mother.

'You could have killed us all, the two of you,' said Mina.

The father got out of the car to talk to the driver of the van. The van had a dent in the side and several long scrapes. 'I'm sorry,' he said. 'That was my fault. I didn't see you coming.'

The van driver shook his head. He was a large man with a gentle face and a drooping moustache. 'These things happen,' he said in his own language. 'You're from another country, not used to these roads.'

'The fault is mine,' said the father in the same language. 'I do not look, I do not see. I regret.'

'Now we have to fill in forms with details of the accident,' said the van driver. He and the father exchanged licences, insurance cards, made notes.

'I knew something was going to happen,' said Mina to Boaz-Jachin. 'I could *feel* it. If my mother and father were sitting in a perfectly stationary box with no wheels and no motor they could make it crash by psychokinesis.'

The car could no longer be driven. The van driver took them and their luggage to a petrol station. Arrangements were made for towing away the car and renting a new one.

'We might as well go to the five-fork-and-spoon place now,' said the father. The van driver offered to take them there, and everybody got into the van but Boaz-Jachin.

'You're invited, you know,' said the father. 'And we'll be going on to the channel port as soon as we get another car.' Please, said the father's eyes, don't leave us yet. Love my daughter for a while. Let her be beautiful for you.

'Thank you very much,' said Boaz-Jachin. 'You've been very generous, but now I want to travel alone again for a while.'

Stay, said the mother's eyes. She can't have her father but she can have you.

Boaz-Jachin kissed Mina goodbye, shook hands with her father and mother while looking away from their eyes. Mina wrote her home address on a piece of paper, tucked it into Boaz-Jachin's pocket. He walked down the road away from the petrol station.

'How do you manage to do it?' he heard Mina ask her parents just before the van started up. 'How do the two of you make everything not be there all of a sudden?'

## 26

Jachin-Boaz was taken to the same hospital where his
wounds had been dressed before. The same doctor saw him
and led him away from the nurse at the admissions desk,
beckoning to the police constable to follow. Gretel stayed
in the waiting room with another constable.

'This is no surprise to me at all,' said the doctor. 'I knew
it would be a matter for the police sooner or later. I suppose
that spiked fence has been after you again, has it?'

'Yes,' said Jachin-Boaz.

'Very well, then,' said the doctor. 'I'm going to be blunt
with you, my good man. If you expect to stay in this
country you'll jolly well have to learn our ways. This
mucking about with large carnivores won't do. Those
animals at the zoo are laid on for the enjoyment of the
general public, and not for the deviant religious practices
of the foreign element.' He turned to the police constable. 'This is the second time he's come in this way, you
know.'

The police constable did not want to be drawn into a
discussion of large carnivores. 'There's a young lady with
him,' he said.

'Of course,' said the doctor. ' "Look for the woman", eh?
Not to put too fine a point on it, there'll be sex at the bottom
of this sort of thing nine times out of ten.' He snipped off
the remnants of Jachin-Boaz's shirt sleeve and swabbed the
wounds with antiseptic. 'Burns a bit, eh?' he said as Jachin-
Boaz went pale. 'You've got some jolly deep bites in you
this time, mate. I don't mind telling you I consider this a

shameful abuse of the National Health Service. I hope there's going to be an inquiry,' he said to the police constable as he medicated and bandaged the wounds.

'Well, we're having him committed for observation of course,' said the constable.

'Use up a little more of the state's money, eh?' said the doctor. 'Everything laid on. Here's this fellow with his cult and his women and his practices ... ' He paused, unbuttoned Jachin-Boaz's shirt, looked for an amulet, found none, and went on, 'And you fetch him in, with a motorcycle escort I shouldn't doubt, and I patch him up, and now he'll have a free holiday in the loony bin. Probably make a few converts there, too. Where'd you find him, and what was going on at the time?'

'On the embankment,' said the constable. 'The lady had a knife.' He met the doctor's eye for a fraction of a second, looked away, encountered Jachin-Boaz's face, looked away again.

'You're not having me on now, are you, old boy?' said the doctor. 'You're not trying to tell me that the lady's knife produces large-carnivore teeth-marks, upper and lower jaws?'

'As you say, this whole thing's got to be looked into,' said the constable. 'If you've finished with him now we'd better be going.'

'Quite,' said the doctor. 'You don't mind giving me your name and number, do you? I'd like to ring up some time just to find out what develops.'

'Not at all,' said the constable. He wrote down his name and number, gave them to the doctor, and took Boaz-Jachin and Gretel to the police station.

At the police station another doctor appeared with a folder in his hand. Gretel waited with the constable while he took Jachin-Boaz into a little office. 'Well, old man,' said the doctor, looking at Jachin-Boaz's bandages, 'been having a little domestic trouble?'

'No,' said Jachin-Boaz.

'What about foreign trouble then?' said the doctor. 'Who's Comrade Lyon?'

'Comrade Lion?' said Jachin-Boaz.

'That's right,' said the doctor. 'A lady who lives on your street reported that she was awakened quite early one morning by your shouting. You were having an argument with Comrade Lyon. He was gone by the time she got to the window, but she's described you accurately. What about that?'

'I don't know,' said Jachin-Boaz.

'Perhaps it was someone else having the argument?'

'I don't know.'

'Hadn't you made a suicide attempt not long before that?'

'Suicide attempt,' Jachin-Boaz repeated. His wounds were very painful, he was very tired, and he wanted more than anything else to lie down and go to sleep.

'The young couple who saw it described to the police a man very like you,' said the doctor. 'They were quite concerned. Actually we ought to have had a talk with you then. Did Comrade Lyon have anything to do with that?'

'There's no Comrade Lion,' said Jachin-Boaz.

'Then whom were you shouting at?'

'I don't know.'

'And what did this unknown person or persons say to you?'

'I don't know,' said Jachin-Boaz. By now the situation felt familiar. The doctor, like the father long ago, was holding up an empty suit of clothes for him to jump into. Jachin-Boaz was too tired not to jump. 'This is what he said,' he told the doctor, and tried to roar. It was not the sound of real anger because he felt no real anger, only a sad and

148

defeated fretfulness, defeated in the foreknowledge that his anger was of no consequence. His feeble roar ended in a fit of coughing. He wiped his eyes, found that he was crying.

'Right,' said the doctor. 'Very good.' He signed the commitment order. Then Jachin-Boaz was taken outside to wait with the constable while Gretel went into the office with the doctor.

'What is your relationship to this man?' said the doctor.
'Close.'
'And your status is what exactly?'
'Working-class. I'm an assistant in a bookshop.'
'Marital status, I mean.'
'I haven't any. I'm a spinster.'
'Do you and this man live together?'
'Yes.'
'Cohabitant,' said the doctor, writing the word as he spoke. 'And what precisely were you doing with the knife?'
'I was co-walking with it.'
'Did you in fact attack this man with the knife?'
'No.'
'Please describe what took place.'
'I can't.'
'Had he been running around with some other woman?'
Gretel stared at him levelly. Her manner of looking at the doctor was like the way she had held the knife that morning. She belonged to a man who had fought with a lion and she carried herself accordingly. The doctor reminded himself that he was the doctor, but felt himself to be less impressive than he would like to be.

'You see two foreigners and immediately the picture is simple for you,' said Gretel. 'Women instead of ladies. Sex, passion, fighting in the street. Hot-blooded foreigners. Bloody cheek!'

The doctor coughed, fleetingly imagined himself involved with Gretel in sex, passion, and fighting in the street. 'Then perhaps you'll tell me what the situation is,' he said with a red face.

'I'm not going to tell you anything at all,' said Gretel, 'and I've no idea what you want with me.'

The doctor reminded himself again that he was the doctor. 'You will allow, madame,' he said stiffly, 'that going about with a knife is rather a dodgy business: one never knows who's going to be injured. I think it might be just as well for you to have some peace and quiet for a few days and think this whole thing over calmly.' He signed the commitment order.

While they waited for the van that would take them to the hospital Jachin-Boaz and Gretel sat down on a bench, and the police constable tactfully walked a few steps away.

Jachin-Boaz sat with tears running down his face. He looked at Gretel, looked away again. His head began to ache. This was somehow her fault. If she hadn't attacked the lion ... No. Before that even. Would the lion have appeared to him if he had not ... No. And of course the lion was in any case his ... what?

The map. Not here. At home, on the desk. In another desk, in the shop where he had once been Jachin-Boaz the map-seller, was a notebook. Were there recent notes in it that were not incorporated in the master-map? The map was on the desk. Were the windows closed? The desk was near the window, and if it rained ... And who would feed the lion?

His mind raced on but he was too tired to pay attention to it any longer. He sat on the bench with both arms bandaged and tears running down his face. Gretel leaned against him, saying nothing.

The police constable indicated that the van was at the

door, and they got into it. Another constable joined them, and the two constables sat across from Jachin-Boaz and Gretel as the van moved away through the daytime streets. Around them flowed the traffic of the ordinary day. Cars and lorries, vans and buses herded together. People on motorcycles and bicycles threaded the narrow spaces between. People walked the pavements, passed in and out of shops, ascended and descended the stairs of underground stations. Aeroplanes flew calmly overhead. Jachin-Boaz sat up straight, craned his neck once to look through the small rear window. A greengrocer in overalls stood under an awning filling a brown paper bag with oranges.

The van stopped, the doors opened. Green shrubbery and lawns appeared around a handsome old red brick building with a white cupola and a gilt weathercock.

Jachin-Boaz and Gretel came out of the van, blinked in the sunlight, walked into the hospital, and were in turn admitted, undressed, examined, drugged, and taken to a men's ward and a women's ward that had the names of trees. In the corridors a smell of cooking wandered like a minstrel of defeat.

Jachin-Boaz, wearing pyjamas and a robe, lay down on his bed. The walls were cream-coloured, the curtains were dark red with yellow-and-blue flowers. There was a long line of beds down each side of the room and french windows that opened on the lawn. The sunlight slanted gently down the walls, not with the harshness of the streets outside. Sunday sunlight. Give up and I'll go easy with you, said the sunlight. Jachin-Boaz fell asleep.

# 27

Boats sink under me, thought Boaz-Jachin. Cars get smashed. At a farm he leaned against a fence and looked into the eyes of a goat. 'What?' he asked the goat. 'Give Urim or give Thummim.' The goat turned away. Goats turn away, thought Boaz-Jachin. The father must live so that the father can die. It became a tune that his mind sang, hurrying him on.

Why am I hurrying? he thought. I've got nothing to do with his living or dying. But hurry was in him. He had no rucksack, no guitar, nothing to carry now. His passport had been in his pocket when the *Swallow* sank. That and the money he had earned on the cruise ship, the new map he had drawn, a toothbrush and the clothes he wore were all he had now. He walked down the road with long strides, going fast, signalling for a ride as he went. Who now? he wondered. Cars, vans, lorries, motorcycles whined, roared, hummed and puttered past.

The van that had taken Mina and her parents to the inn pulled up beside him. The large gentle face of the driver looked out of the window, spoke as a question the name of a channel port. Boaz-Jachin repeated the name, said, 'Yes.' The driver opened the door and he got in.

In his own language the driver said, 'I don't suppose you speak my language.'

Boaz-Jachin smiled, lifted his shoulders, shook his head. 'I don't speak your language,' he said in English.

'That's what I thought,' said the driver, understanding the gesture rather than the words. He nodded, sighed, and settled down to his driving. Ahead of them the numberless grains of the road flowed into sharp focus, rolled beneath the wheels, spun out behind.

'All the same,' said the driver, 'I feel like talking.'

'I know what you mean,' said Boaz-Jachin, understanding the voice but not the words. Now he spoke not English but his own language, and his voice was more subtly inflected. 'I feel like talking too.'

'You too,' said the driver. 'So we'll talk. It'll be just as good as many of the conversations I've had with people who spoke the same language. After all, when you come right down to it, how many people speak the same language even when they speak the same language?'

'After all,' said Boaz-Jachin, 'it won't be the first time I've spoken to someone who couldn't understand what I was saying. And when you come right down to it, how many people speak the same language even when they speak the same language?'

They looked at each other, shrugged, raised their eyebrows.

'That's how it is,' said the driver.

'That's how it is,' said Boaz-Jachin.

'Empty space,' said the driver. 'There's a funny thing to think about. The back of the van is full of empty space. I brought it from my town. But I've opened the doors several times since I left. So is it still empty space from my town or is it now several different new empty spaces? This is the sort of thing one thinks about sometimes. If the back of the van were full of chairs the question wouldn't arise. One assumes that the space between the chairs remains the same all through the trip. Empty space, however, is something else.'

Boaz-Jachin nodded, understanding not a word. But the driver's voice, large and gentle like the rest of him, was agreeable to him. He felt very conversational with him.

'I offered the drawings,' he said, surprised to hear himself saying it but pleased with what he was saying. 'I offered the drawings. I burned the drawings. Something went out of me, leaving an empty space in me. Sometimes I feel myself hurrying towards something up ahead. What? I'm a rushing empty space. The father must live so that the father can die. Are you a father? Certainly you're a son. Every man who is alive is a son. Dead men as well are sons. Dead fathers too are sons. No end to it.'

'You're young,' said the driver. 'Your whole life is ahead of you. Probably you don't think about such things. Did I when I was your age? I can't remember. Yet I suppose there must be empty space in you. What will you put into it?'

'The space wasn't always empty,' said Boaz-Jachin. 'Only after the offering of the drawings. Now I'm hurrying. To what? Why? I don't know. Lion. I haven't said that aloud very often, that word, that name. Lion. Lion, lion, lion. What? Where?' He leaned forward, leaning into the forward speed of the van. 'That he took the master-map he'd promised to me, what's that to me? I don't need it. Maps.' From his pocket he took the new one he'd sketched on the cruise ship, opened the window, started to throw it away, put it back in his pocket, closed the window. 'I'll keep it the way people keep diaries, but I don't need maps for finding anything.' He ground his teeth, wanted to roar, wanted to do violence to something.

'Years and years,' said Boaz-Jachin. 'My eyes only as high as the edge of the table. "Let me help," I said. "Let me work on a little corner." No. Nothing. He wouldn't let me. I couldn't make clean beautiful lines. Always he had to do the whole thing. He looked at me but he spoke to a place where I wasn't. "You will not follow me into the shop," he said. "For you there is the whole world outside." Fine. Good.

154

Go into the wide world. Go away. I wasn't good enough to work with him. So now *he* goes into the wide world. The shop for him and the world for him. For me nothing.' He ground his teeth again. 'I have to ... What? What do I have to do? I have to tell him ... What? What do I have to tell him? Benjamin's father wrote *forgive*. Forgive whom what? What is it to forgive? Who has forgiveness to give? He held up a suit of clothes for me to jump into: the wanderer. Here's your map. Then he ran away with the map. I jumped into the wandering clothes. Is he happy now?' Tears streamed down Boaz-Jachin's cheeks.

'Name of God,' said the driver. 'What an outburst! After all that surely there must be empty space inside you. My word. There's something about a road. One thinks, one talks. The van eats up the miles, the soul eats up the miles. At the port I'm picking up some wooden crates. In the crates is the machinery for a new press for the local newspaper. The editor's wife ran off with a salesman. So he needs new machinery. That's reasonable. With his new machinery he will print the news. This one is born, that one died, so-and-so is opening a bakery. Maybe even the news that he is married again. All of this comes out of what is now an empty space. There are depths in this. It's a lot to think about. From an empty space the future. If there's no empty space where can one put the future? It all figures if you take the time to think it out. It's a pleasure talking with you. It's doing me a lot of good.'

Boaz-Jachin wiped his eyes, blew his nose. 'It's a pleasure talking with you,' he said. 'It's doing me a lot of good.'

# 28

The man in the bed next to Jachin-Boaz was sitting up crosslegged, writing on a foolscap pad a letter to the editor of the city's leading newspaper. *'With our Sanitation Department on the job regularly cleaning the streets,'* he wrote, *'is it not astonishing that so far no measures have been taken towards resolving the problem of image accumulation? The private citizen, however diligently he may divest his home of mirrors and however carefully he may cover windows and polished tables, has daily to encounter public mirrors, shop windows, and innumerable reflecting surfaces from which decades and scores of years of faces, his own and those of strangers, peer out impertinently to mock him.*

*'As a law-abiding citizen and ratepayer ...* ' He stopped writing. He had been aware of figures moving past his bed towards the french windows, and now he looked up. Three patients were standing at the windows looking out at the lawn. Two male nurses who had been sitting in chairs stood up, looked out, and sat down again.

The letter writer got out of bed and walked over to the group at the window, sensing at once that they shared a secret from which the nurses were excluded. He too looked out for a time at the lawn that was green and golden in the afternoon sunlight. Then he came back and sat down on the edge of his bed, looking at the sleeping Jachin-Boaz. He stared at him fixedly, and after half an hour Jachin-Boaz opened his eyes.

'Is it yours?' said the letter writer. 'It must be—you're the only new arrival.' He had a small aristocratic moustache and goatee. His eyes were pale blue and very sharp. 'What do you feed it?'

Jachin-Boaz smiled and lifted his eyebrows interrogatively. The powerful tranquillizing-drug dose had left him sluggish, and the question did not immediately make itself clear to him.

'The lion,' said the letter writer, and saw Jachin-Boaz look somewhat more alert. 'It *is* your lion, isn't it? It seems to have arrived with you.'

'It's here?' said Jachin-Boaz.

'Walking about on the lawn,' said the letter writer.

'Everybody sees it?' said Jachin-Boaz.

'Only a few of us. Those who did and were on the lawn when it appeared came inside directly. Some of the staff and a number of pseudo-nuts are still outside with it, quite blind to its existence. I must say it seems a well-behaved animal. It isn't bothering anyone.'

'I don't think it takes notice of everybody,' said Jachin-Boaz.

'Naturally not. Who does?' said the letter writer. 'As I was saying, what do you feed it?'

Jachin-Boaz became wary and sly. Hold on to everything you have, said the sunlight slanting down the wall. He didn't want anyone else to know what or how much his lion ate. 'How do you know it eats?' he said.

The letter writer's face flushed. He looked as if he had been struck. 'I'm so sorry,' he said. 'I beg your pardon.'

In a flash Jachin-Boaz understood that it was as if one duke who owned a rare and expensive motorcar had been rude to another duke who happened not to own such a car. He blushed. 'Forgive me,' he said. 'He should have six or seven pounds of meat a day, six days a week. I've been feeding him beefsteak, but not regularly.'

'Something of a supply problem,' said the letter writer cosily. 'I don't suppose that he could accustom himself to shepherd's pie and toad-in-the-hole? Meat is a bit thin on the ground here.'

'I don't know,' said Jachin-Boaz. 'Actually, it may even be possible that he can do without food altogether. He's real enough, but not in the ordinary way.'

'Quite,' said the letter writer stiffly, as between dukes to whom such things need not be explained.

Jachin-Boaz fell silent. He did not want to see the lion just now, and he began to think about the other people who could see it. Already this other man wanted to feed it. Jachin-Boaz began to get a headache. 'Why can they see it, the others?' he said, speaking to himself but saying the words aloud.

'Sorry about that, old man,' said the letter writer. 'But you've got to expect that sort of thing here. After all, why have they put us in the fun house? The straight people agree that some things are not allowed to be possible, and they govern their perceptions accordingly. Very strong, the straight people. We're not so strong as they. Things not allowed to be possible jump on us, beasts and demons, because we don't know how to keep them out.

'Others here can see my faces and they can see your lion, even though you may want to hug it to yourself like a teddy bear. If your lion weren't possible you'd be happy to share the impossibility. But people get very possessive about possibilities, even dangerous ones. Victims become proprietors. You may have to grow up a little. Perhaps you'll even have to let go of your lion one day.'

'And your faces?' said Jachin-Boaz.

'They accumulate faster than they can be taken away,' said the letter writer smugly. 'There'll always be more.'

'Lovely,' said the man who had just returned to the bed

on the other side. Empty-handed and in bathrobe and pyjamas, he appeared to be fully and impeccably dressed and carrying a tightly furled umbrella and a respectable newspaper. 'Lovely,' he continued. 'Lovely wife, children, home, weather, central heating, career, garden, shoelaces, buttons and dentistry. All modern conveniences, or nearest offer. Lovely bank lessons, music account, lovely miles to the gallon. Lovely 'O' Levels, 'A' Levels, eye levels, level eyes. Lovely level eyes she has and sees through everything but.'

'But what?' said Jachin-Boaz.

'That's what I mean,' said the tightly furled man. 'The butness of everything. I don't go home any more. Goodbye, little yellow bird. That's the cracks of it, sweetheart.'

'Crux,' said Jachin-Boaz.

'Show me a crux and I'll show you the cracks,' said the tightly furled man. 'You're not talking to squares now, darling. Don't try to slide by on crossword puzzles and ninety-nine-year leases. The blank spaces are bigger than ziggurats here, and it's a long long climb. Deeper than a well.'

'Rounder than a wheel?' said Jachin-Boaz.

'You're forcing it, poppet,' said the tightly furled man. 'Just let it happen.'

'Don't be a snob,' said Jachin-Boaz.

'Look who's talking,' said the tightly furled man. 'Him with his lions and his traveller's cheques and his cameras. Obesity is the mother of distension. A bitch in time shaved mine. Take the bleeding castles apart and ship them home stone by stone for all I care. Piss off, you and your lion both. Tourists.'

'There's no need to take that tone,' said Jachin-Boaz.

The tightly furled man began to cry. Kneeling on the bed, he bent forward, burying his head in his arms, thrusting out his bottom. 'I didn't mean it,' he said. 'Let me pet the lion. He can eat my dinner every day.'

Jachin-Boaz turned away, lay back on his bed with his arms behind his head and stared straight up at the ceiling, attempting to find silence and privacy in the space over him that was presumably as wide as his bed, as high as the room, and his personal domain. The sunlight said, Once you begin to doubt you will lose everything. Begin now. 'No,' said Jachin-Boaz to the curtains. You will perish, said the red, said the yellow-and-blue flowers. We abide. Many have come and gone here, said the smell of cooking. All have been defeated.

Jachin-Boaz became aware that someone with mental-hospital-doctor feet had arrived at his bed. He had sometimes heard clocks whose tick-tocks became words. When the doctor spoke, his words became tick-tocks unless Jachin-Boaz listened very hard.

'How are we tick-tock today?' said the doctor. 'Tick-tock?'

'Very tock, thank you,' said Jachin-Boaz.

'Tick,' said the doctor. 'Ticks will tock themselves out, I have no doubt.'

'I tick so,' said Jachin-Boaz.

'Tick all right last tock?'

'Very tock,' said Jachin-Boaz. 'No dreams that I can remember forgetting.'

'That's the ticket,' said the doctor. 'Tock it tick.'

'Cheers,' said Jachin-Boaz, making an upward gesture with two fingers.

'You do it the other way for victory,' said the doctor.

'When I see a victory I'll do it that way,' said Jachin-Boaz.

The doctor's feet went away, and the doctor went with them. Civilian feet appeared. Familiar shoes.

'How are you feeling?' said the owner of the bookshop. 'Are you all right?'

'Not so bad, thank you,' said Jachin-Boaz. 'It's kind of you to come.'

'How come you're here?' said the bookshop owner. 'You seem the same as you've always been. Was it the dog-food-eating hallucination?'

'Something like that,' said Jachin-Boaz. 'Unfortunately a police constable saw it too.'

'Ah,' said the bookshop owner. 'It's always best to keep that sort of thing to yourself, you know.'

'I should like to have kept it to myself,' said Jachin-Boaz.

'Things'll sort themselves out,' said the bookshop owner. 'The rest will do you good and you'll come back to work refreshed.'

'You don't have any reservations about taking me back?' said Jachin-Boaz.

'Why should I? You sell more books than any other assistant I've ever had. Anybody can come unstuck once in a while.'

'Thank you.'

'Not at all. Oh, there was an advert in the trade weekly. Letter for you at a box number. Here it is.'

'A letter for me,' said Jachin-Boaz. He opened the envelope. In it was another envelope, postmarked at his town, his town where he had been Jachin-Boaz the map-seller. 'Thank you,' he said, and put the letter on his bedside table.

'And here's some fruit,' said the bookshop owner, 'and a couple of paperbacks.'

'Thank you,' said Jachin-Boaz. He took an orange from the bag, held it in his hand. The paperbacks were two collections of supernatural and horror stories.

'Escape literature,' said the bookshop owner.

'Escape,' said Jachin-Boaz.

'I'll stop in again,' said the bookshop owner. 'Get well soon.'

'Yes,' said Jachin-Boaz. 'Thank you.'

# 29

Only you, said the black water rushing past the ferry in the night.

'Only I what, for God's sake!' said Boaz-Jachin. He saw no one near him, and spoke aloud. He leaned over the rail, smelled the blackness of the sea and cursed the water. 'Every fucking thing talks to me,' he said. 'Leave me alone for a while. I'll talk to you some other time. I can't be rushed all the time.' He walked aft to the stern, saw flights of white gulls rising and falling in eerie silence above the wake. Out of the darkness into the light. Out of the light into the darkness. Boaz-Jachin shook his fist at the gulls. 'I don't even know if he's there!' he said. 'I don't even know if I'm looking for him in the right place.'

You know, said the white wings silently rising and falling. Don't tell us you don't know.

'That's what I'm telling you,' said Boaz-Jachin leaning out over the rail. 'I *don't* know.' He saw no one on the afterdeck, and he began to talk more loudly, to shout into the darkness and the wake. 'I don't know! I don't know!' Two gulls slanted towards each other like eyebrows, became for a moment a pale frown following the boat. Boaz-Jachin put one foot on the bottom rail and leaned farther out, staring at the darkness where the white wings had crossed and separated.

He felt a hand gripping his belt from behind. He turned, and was face to face with a woman. His turning had brought her arm halfway around him and their faces close together. She did not let go of his belt.

163

'What's the matter?' said Boaz-Jachin.

'Come away from the rail,' she said, still holding his belt. Her voice was one that he had heard before. They moved towards the lighted windows of the lounge, and he saw her face clearly.

'You!' he said.

'You know me?'

'You gave me a ride. Months ago it was, on the other side, on the road to the port. You had a red car with a tape machine playing music. You didn't like the way I looked at you.'

She let go of his belt. Under his shirt his flesh burned where her arm had been around him.

'I didn't recognize you,' she said.

'Why did you grab me by the belt?'

'It made me nervous to see you leaning out over the rail that way and shouting into the dark.'

'You thought I was going to jump overboard?'

'It made me nervous, that's all. You look older.'

'You look kinder.'

She smiled, took his arm, walked with him along the deck past the lighted windows. Her breast against his arm made it feel hot.

'*Did* you think I was going to jump overboard?' said Boaz-Jachin.

'I have a son about your age,' she said.

'Where is he?'

'I don't know. I never hear from him.'

'Where's your husband?'

'With a new wife.'

They walked the deck all the way around the boat, then around again. Hearing her say that her husband was with a new wife was not the same to Boaz-Jachin as the word *divorcée* that had been in his mind that day on the road.

'You've changed,' she said. 'You're less of a boy.'

'More of a man?'

'More of a person. More of a man.'

They drank cognac in the bar. In a corridor a group of students with back packs sang while one of them played a guitar. Honey, let me be your salty dog, went the song.

When the boat docked they drove off in the little red car. 'Purpose of your visit?' said the customs officer as he looked at Boaz-Jachin's passport.

'Holiday,' said Boaz-Jachin. The customs officer looked at his face and his black hair, then at the blonde woman. He stamped the passport, handed it back.

It was raining, drumming on the canvas top. Numberless splashes leaped up from the road to meet the rain coming down. Red tail-lights blurred ahead of them. Yes, no, yes, no, said the windscreen wipers. The woman put a cassette in the machine. Where the morning sees the shadows of the orange grove there was nothing twenty years ago, sang the tape in the language of Boaz-Jachin's country. Where the dry wind sowed the desert we brought water, planted seedlings, now the oranges grow. A woman's voice, harsh and full of glaring sunlight.

Benjamin, thought Boaz-Jachin. Forgive. 'You can buy that on a cassette?' he said.

'Sure,' she said.

Boaz-Jachin shook his head. Why not thought cassettes too? Any kind. What an invention. A slot in the head and you just put in the cassette for the mood you wanted. Lion. Yes, I know, thought Boaz-Jachin. You're in my mind. I'm in your mind.

'Oranges,' said the woman. 'Oranges in the desert.' She looked straight ahead into the darkness and the red tail-lights and drove on through the rain. For an hour they said nothing.

165

She turned off the main road, drove two or three miles to a half-timbered cottage with a thatched roof. Boaz-Jachin looked at her.

'Yes,' she said. 'Houses. Houses I have. Three of them in different countries.' She looked at his face. 'Last time in the car you were thinking of a hotel, weren't you?'

Boaz-Jachin blushed.

She lit lamps, took covers off the furniture in the living room, went into the kitchen to make coffee. Boaz-Jachin took kindling from a basket, coal from a scuttle, started a fire in the fireplace. The books on the shelves came and went in the firelight, red, brown, orange, all their pages quiet. Thin gleams of gold showed in the insets of picture frames. Boaz-Jachin smelled coffee, looked at the couch, looked away, looked at the fire, sat in a chair, sighed.

They drank coffee. She smoked cigarettes. The silence sat down with them like an invisible creature with its finger to its lips. They looked at the fire. The silence looked at the fire. The fire seethed and whispered. They were both sitting on the floor, on an oriental carpet. Boaz-Jachin looked at the pattern, the asymmetry of the endings of rows and the border. He covered the asymmetry between them by moving close to her. He kissed her, feeling as if he might be struck dead by lightning. She unbuttoned his shirt.

When they were both naked her body was surprising. It was as if not being allowed to be a wife had kept her flesh firm and young. Boaz-Jachin was staggered by the unbelievable reality of what was happening. Again, said the backs of the books, the golden gleams in the picture frames.

My God, thought Boaz-Jachin, and led her to the couch. She turned and hit him in the jaw. She was strong, and it was not a woman's blow. She pivoted athletically, like a boxer, and hit him with her feet planted solidly and all of her weight behind her fist. Boaz-Jachin saw shooting coloured lights, then everything went black for a moment as he flew across the room and fetched up in an armchair. He was speechless.

He stood up shakily. Naked she came towards him and hit him in the stomach. All the breath went out of him as she brought up her knee. Blackness and coloured lights again, pain and nausea. Boaz-Jachin, rolling on the floor, caught her ankle as she tried to heel-kick him. He pulled, and she came down hard with a thump and a little scream. He crawled over to her on his hands and knees, struck her hard across the face with a backhanded blow. She rolled over on to her side, drew up her knees and lay there crying while her nose bled.

Boaz-Jachin lay beside her until the pain and nausea went away. Then he got up, stirred her with his foot, helped her up, led her to the couch, mounted her as one who had arrived with chariots and spears, and took his pleasure.

'You,' she said into his ear. 'Oranges in the desert.'

In the morning there was sunlight. He felt deathless, invincible, the initiate of mysteries, blessed.

# 30

It would be better for me not to open this letter, thought Jachin-Boaz as he opened the letter. Fading, fading, said the afternoon sunlight slanting down the wall, slanting on the red curtains, on the yellow, on the blue of the flowers. See how tactfully I die! said the sunlight. Twilight follows. Fade with me.

Jachin-Boaz began to read. In the next bed the letter writer was hard at work. *Violet's face, for instance,* he wrote. *Is there, in all justice, any necessity for that? She married the young lieutenant to whom I'd introduced her. Everyone said the baby looked exactly like him. Yet only this morning there was Violet's face in a spoon. Not a silver spoon either. Not even a clean spoon, mind you.*

On the other side the tightly furled man was looking at a magazine in which girls in black suspender belts and stockings achieved difficult juxtapositions. He was quietly singing *Oft in the Stilly Night* in a high falsetto.

The letter writer looked up. The tightly furled man put down his magazine, left off singing. Jachin-Boaz had put the letter in the drawer of his bedside table, flung himself back on his bed, and lay looking up at the ceiling in a silence that filled the air with waves of terror. The two men on either side felt as if they had been fused with the sounding metal of some monstrous bell that was rhythmically annihilating them.

'Stop clanging, can't you?' said the tightly furled man. 'It's driving the very marrow out of my bones.' He doubled up in his bed and covered his ears.

'Really,' said the letter writer to Jachin-Boaz, 'I think you might have the civility not to indulge in effects like that. I can hear mirrors shattering for miles around. Do make an effort, won't you?'

'I'm sorry,' said Jachin-Boaz. 'I didn't know that I was doing anything.' Bad heart, she said. His father had died of a bad heart and he had a bad heart too. He *had* had twinges now and then, and his doctor had pointed out that he was a cardiac type and would do well to be careful. Suddenly he felt his heart clearly defined in his body, totally vulnerable and waiting for the inevitable. Angina pectoris. Had the doctor said anything about that? He'd looked it up once. Something associated with apprehension or fear of impending death, said the dictionary. He must remember not to be apprehensive or fearful of impending death. He closed his eyes, and in his mind he saw the map of his body with the organs, nerves and circulatory system illuminated in vivid colour. The heart pumped, drove the blood through the branching veins and arteries. Around went the blood on the animated map, and around again. It seemed miraculous that the heart kept pumping. How had it continued twenty-four hours a day for forty-seven years? It could never stop for a rest. When it stopped that was the end of everything. No more world. Only a few years left, suddenly they will all be gone, the last moment will be now. Intolerable! Father died at fifty-two. I'm forty-seven. Five more years? Less, perhaps.

You will want to come back to me.

Yes, I do want to come back. Why did I want to go away? What was so bad? Certainly I never felt *this* bad before.

The letter writer and the tightly furled man got up and went to the lounge. Jachin-Boaz went to one of the nurses, asked for something to calm him down. He was given a tranquillizer, went back to his bed and reasoned with himself.

She can't actually make my heart stop, he thought. That kind of magic doesn't work unless you believe that the other person has the power. Do I believe she has the power? Yes. But she doesn't really have any special power. She didn't have the power to keep me, did she? No. Then could she have the power to kill me? Of course not. Do I believe that? No.

Jachin-Boaz lay with his ear to the pillow, listening to the beating of his heart. The map, he thought. The map of Boaz-Jachin's future that I stole, the future that I cannot have. I'll stop smoking.

He lit a cigarette, got out of bed, stood against the wall. As soon as I feel a little better, he thought, I'll stop smoking. My father with his cigars. Why did she have to tell me about the mistress? She found out from her aunt in the dramatic society, but why did she have to tell me?

He thought of Sunday afternoons in childhood, smelled the car upholstery, looked out through the windscreen at the waning sunlight, felt his father on one side, his mother on the other, himself between them, sick. I haven't been committing suicide, he thought. Suicide has been committing me.

All of his unremembered dreams seemed to walk silently behind him, passing one by one between him and the wall, smirking over his shoulder at invisible phantoms in front of him. If I turn very quickly, he thought, and turned. Something very big, something very small, whisked around the corner of his mind. Either way, said the answer in the wall that faced him: betrayed or betrayer. Betrayed *and* betrayer.

'Be reasonable,' said Jachin-Boaz quietly to the wall. 'I can't be everybody.'

Loss unending, said the wall. Dare to let go?

'I don't know,' said Jachin-Boaz.

Suppose, the wall said, sometimes he laughed away from home. What then? You owe her nothing. He wants to rest. If you stand up they lie down. Follow your noes.

'Lion,' said Jachin-Boaz silently, only shaping the word.

Oh yes, the wall said. Play with yourself.

Jachin-Boaz turned away. Everyone else was going to dinner. The thought of food sickened him, the smell from the dining area was offensive. The lion was still outside, no doubt. He would be waiting all the time now until the end. Everybody would want to feed him, look at him, share him. No, no, no.

The tightly furled man had taken his plate to the door near the french windows. 'Pss, pss,' he called, making the sound one makes for a cat. Three others came and stood near, looking over his shoulder. One of them, a man with a round white face, looked back at Jachin-Boaz and said something to the others. Everyone laughed.

Jachin-Boaz felt immensities of rage in him, infinities of NO. Crying, he burst into the group by the door, flung them in all directions, and rushed out on to the lawn.

# 3I

Boaz-Jachin had arrived in the city and was staying with friends of the blonde woman. When he told them that his father was likely to be selling maps they advised him to advertise for Jachin-Boaz in the book trade weekly, which he did.

Boaz-Jachin bought such clothes as he needed and a cheap guitar, and every day he went into the underground stations and sang and played. The money he had earned on the cruise ship would keep him for several months, but he wanted to be able to support himself for as long as he needed to remain in the city.

His advertisement would not appear until the next week, and while he waited he played his guitar and sang in two different stations every day. He timed his arrival so that he would be at one when people went to work and at the other when they went home. Each day he went to new stations in the hope of seeing Jachin-Boaz. Each station had its own sound and its own feel. Some felt as if Jachin-Boaz was not to be found in them, others seemed full of probability. Boaz-Jachin made a list of the latter. If there was no answer to the advertisement he would keep only those stations on his guitar route as time went on.

The advertisement appeared, but there were no telephone calls or letters for Boaz-Jachin at the house where he was staying. He went on with his guitar route, trying new stations daily. He made enough money to live on cheaply, found a room for himself, and settled down to stay until he found his father. He no longer asked himself whether he knew or how he knew that Jachin-Boaz was in this city. He felt it as a certainty. Every day he inquired for letters or telephone calls, and every day there was nothing.

Boaz-Jachin's ear became attuned to the roar of trains arriving and departing, the constant numberless footfalls approaching, receding, voices and echoes. He sang the songs of his country, sang of the well, of olives, of sheep in the hills, of the desert, of orange groves, his voice and his guitar echoing in the corridors and stairways under the ground in the great city.

Boaz-Jachin inserted another advertisement, subscribed to the trade weekly, and went on to new underground stations with his guitar. He became known to his regular clientele. At each station the same faces smiled at him day after day as coins dropped into the guitar case. He smiled back, said thank you, but said nothing else to anyone. In the morning he saw the daylight and in the evenings he saw the fading of it. Above him the city was immense with all that the lines on the master-map led to. Bridges crossed the river, birds flew up circling over squares, and Boaz-Jachin lived underground, singing in corridors and stairways. He had not spoken aloud the word *lion* since the ride to the channel port with the van driver.

Boaz-Jachin found that he was thinking less in words than he used to. His mind simply was, and in it were the people he had been with, the times he had lived. Sounds, voices, faces, bodies, places, light and darkness came and went.

He had no sexual appetite, wanted no one to talk to, read nothing. Often in the evenings he sat quietly in his room doing nothing. Sometimes he played the guitar quietly, improvising tunes, but more often he had no wish to let out anything that was in him, nor did he look for anything new to take in. Whatever thoughts and questions were in his mind carried on their own dialogues to which he paid little attention. The feeling of emptiness rushing towards something became a waiting stillness.

Sometimes at night he walked in the streets. The leaves of the trees rustled in the squares. Lights shone on statues. Often he seemed to be without thought. It ceased to matter to him who was looking out through the eyeholes in his face and it ceased to matter who was looking in. He had no amulet to wear around his neck, no magic stone to hold in his hand. He held nothing. He was. Time passed through him unimpeded.

One day Boaz-Jachin took his guitar to an underground station, put the open case on the floor beside him, and tuned the instrument. But he did not begin to play immediately.

Faces passed him. Footsteps echoed, pattering like rain. Trains came and went. Boaz-Jachin listened past the footsteps, past the trains and echoes to the silence. He began to play music of his own, improvising on themes that he had composed in his room. He was unwilling to let the music out of him but unable to make himself stop.

He played the shimmer of the heat on the plains and the motion of the running flickering on the dry wind, tawny, great, and quickly gone. He played the silence of a ghost roar on the rising air beneath a shivering honey-coloured moon.

He played lion-music, and he sang. He sang without words, sang only with the modulations of his voice rising and falling, light and dark in the dry wind, in the sunlit desert under the ground in the great city.

Beyond the footsteps, beyond the trains and echoes he heard a roar that flooded the corridors like a great river of lion-coloured sound. He heard the lion.

# 32

No lion. Nothing. A faint smell of hot sun, dry wind. The green lawn darkening, empty in the twilight. Ha ha, said the twilight. Fading, fading.

Jachin-Boaz stood on the empty lawn with his fists clenched. I might have known, he thought. I was there, I was ready, high on a great cresting wave. Gone. The chance missed. He's gone. I won't see him again.

He went slowly back inside. The men who had laughed by the door looked at him warily from a distance.

'How're we feeling?' said one of the male nurses, laying a heavy hand on his shoulder. 'We're not going to be acting up any more this evening, are we? We don't want to be plugged into the wall, do we? Because a little E.C.T.-time is just the ticket for smoothing out the wrinkles in our brow and settling us down nicely.'

'Feeling fine,' said Jachin-Boaz. 'No more acting up. All settled down. Don't know why I made such a fuss.'

'Lovely,' said the nurse, squeezing the back of Jachin-Boaz's neck. 'Good boy.'

Jachin-Boaz walked slowly back to his bed, sat down. 'What's E.C.T.?' he asked the letter writer.

'Electro-convulsion therapy. Shock treatment. It's lovely. From time to time when the faces get too many for me I act up and they let me have it. Ever so soothing.'

'You like it?' said Jachin-Boaz.

'Can't really afford any other kind of a holiday, you know,' said the letter writer. 'It scrambles the brain nicely. One forgets a good deal. Sometimes it takes months for

everything to come back. Everyone ought to have a portable
E.C.T. box, like a transistor radio. It isn't fair to leave a chap
all alone and unprotected at the mercy of a brain. Brains
don't care about you, you know. They do just as they like,
and there you are.'

'Transistor, transbrothers, transfathers, transmothers,'
said the tightly furled man. 'Real rock. Groovy. "No motion
has she now, no force; She neither hears nor sees; Roll'd
round in earth's diurnal course, With rocks, and stones, and
trees." Sometimes there's nothing but Sundays for weeks on
end. Why can't they move Sunday to the middle of the
week so you could put it in the OUT tray on your desk?
No. Bloody bastards. Let the shadow cabinet work on
*that* for a while, and the substance cabinet too. Man is a
product of his Sundays. Don't talk to me about heredity.
Darwin went to the Galapagos to get away from the
Sunday drive with his parents. Mendel pea'd. Everybody
tells a boy about sex but nobody tells him the facts of Sunday.
Home is where the heart is, that's why pubs stay in business.
Forgive us our Sundays as we forgive those who Sunday
against us. Parent or child, no difference. Lend me a Monday,
for Christ's sake.' He began to cry.

'Today isn't Sunday,' said Jachin-Boaz.

'Yes it is,' said the tightly furled man. 'It's always Sunday. That's why business was invented—to give people
offices to hide in five days a week. Give us a seven-day week,
I say. It's getting worse all the time. Inhuman bastards.
Where'd your lion go?'

'Away,' said Jachin-Boaz. 'He won't come back. He
only shows up on weekdays, and it's always Sunday here.'
He smiled cruelly, and the tightly furled man cried harder
and burrowed into the blankets and covered up his head.

There would be no more lion for him here, Jachin-Boaz
knew. The great cresting wave of rage had not been

honestly earned, had been artificially forced up in him by the sly teasing of those who had no lion of their own. He would have to be good, be quiet, muffle his terror and wait for his rage until he was out of here. He would have to hide the clanging in him when it came again, would have to wear his terror like quiet grey prison garb, let everything flow through him indifferently.

From that time on his walk became like that of many other patients. Even when wearing shoes he seemed to go barefoot, ungirded, disarmed. The smell of cooking sang defeat. He nodded, humbled.

'How's it ticking?' said the doctor when his feet brought him around to Jachin-Boaz again.

'Very well, thank you,' said Jachin-Boaz. From now on he would remember to answer as if the doctor were speaking real words.

'Tockly,' said the doctor. 'I told you ticks would tock themselves out, didn't I?'

'Indeed you did,' said Jachin-Boaz. 'And you were right.'

'Someticks all it tocks is a little tick,' said the doctor. 'My tockness, ticks get to be too tock for all of us someticks.'

'They do,' said Jachin-Boaz.

'Tick,' said the doctor. 'That's when a good tock and some tick and tocket will tick tockers, and then a fellow can tick himtock toticker.'

'Right,' said Jachin-Boaz. 'Peace and quiet *will* work wonders, and I *am* pulling myself together.'

'That's the ticket,' said the doctor. 'We'll tick you out of tock in no tick.'

'The sooner the better,' said Jachin-Boaz.

'What's all this about lions then?' said the doctor with every word clear and distinct.

'Who said anything about lions?' said Jachin-Boaz.

'It's difficult to have any secrets in a place like this,' said the doctor. 'Word gets around pretty quickly.'

'I may very well have said something about a lion at one time or another,' said Jachin-Boaz. 'But if I did I was speaking metaphorically. It's very easy to be misunderstood, you know. Especially in a place like this.'

'Quite,' said the doctor. 'Nothing easier. But what about the bites and the claw-marks?'

'Well,' said Jachin-Boaz, 'everyone's entitled to his own sex life, I think. Some people fancy black rubber clothes. Consenting adults and all that is how I feel about it.'

'Quite,' said the doctor. 'The thing is to keep it in the privacy of one's own home, you know. I'm as modern as anyone else, but it's got to be kept off the streets.'

'You're right of course,' said Jachin-Boaz. 'Things get out of hand sometimes.'

'But the claw-marks and the bites,' said the doctor. 'They certainly weren't made by any human partner.'

'Animal skins', said Jachin-Boaz, 'can be got with claws and teeth, you know. It's been disposed of since. Really, I'm terribly ashamed of the whole thing. I just want to get back to my job and settle down to a normal life again.'

'Good,' said the doctor. 'That's the way to talk. It won't be long now.'

Gretel came to visit Jachin-Boaz. He had scarcely thought of her since being admitted to the hospital and would have preferred not to have to think about her just now. He was amazed at how young and pretty she was. My woman, he thought. How did it happen? It's dangerous to have balls but there's something nice about it.

'They're letting me out tomorrow,' she said.

'What did you tell them?' said Jachin-Boaz.

'I said that it was all sex. You know how it is with us hot-blooded foreigners. I said that I thought you were

178

running around with other women and that my jealousy had driven me wild and that somehow I found myself in the street with a knife in my hand.'

'And they're willing to let you go?'

'Well, I said that I mightn't have been so upset ordinarily, but being pregnant as I was it was all too much for me. And the doctor said oh well, of course, poor dear and unwed mother and all that. And the doctor said what about the father, and I said not to worry, that everything was all right but we couldn't get married until you had a divorce. And he patted my hand and wished me all the best and said he hoped I'd not be going about with knives any more and I said certainly not and they're letting me out tomorrow.'

'That was a very good touch, the pregnancy,' said Jachin-Boaz.

'Yes,' said Gretel. 'It was. I am.'

'Am what?'

'Pregnant.'

'Pregnant,' said Jachin-Boaz.

'That's right. I was two weeks overdue and had a test just before coming to the loony bin. I never found an opportune moment to tell you about it the day they brought us in. Are you happy about it?'

'Good God,' said Jachin-Boaz. 'Another son.'

'It could also be a girl.'

'I doubt it. With me it'll always be fathers and sons, I think.'

'What I said about getting married, you know, was just for the doctor. I don't care about that.'

'It's something we have to think about, I guess,' said Jachin-Boaz.

'We don't have to think about it right now, anyhow,' said Gretel. 'How do you feel about being a father again?'

'I'm happy about the baby,' said Jachin-Boaz. 'I don't

know how I feel about being a father again. I don't know how I feel about being a father even once, let alone twice.'

'It'll be all right, whatever happens,' said Gretel. 'A mighty fortress is our something.'

'What do you mean, whatever happens?'

'If you leave me. Or if the lion … '

'Do you think I'll leave you?'

'I never know. But it doesn't matter. I'll love you anyhow, and so will the baby. I'll tell him about his father, and he'll love you too.'

'Do you think the lion will kill me?'

'Do you want the lion to kill you?'

Jachin-Boaz looked at Gretel without answering.

'What is there to say about a lion?' she said. 'There are no lions any more, but my man has a lion. The father of my child has a lion.'

Jachin-Boaz nodded his head.

'Maybe,' said Gretel, 'if you go out to meet it again … '

'I'll tell you,' said Jachin-Boaz.

'All right,' said Gretel. 'When I get home I'll do some house-cleaning so the flat can welcome you properly. You'll be out soon, I should think. I shan't come to visit unless you ring me up. You have a lot to think about.'

'I do,' said Jachin-Boaz. He kissed her. My woman, he thought. The mother of my child. I'm an unwed father, and my heart may stop beating at any moment.

The owner of the bookshop came to visit Jachin-Boaz again. 'You're getting to be quite popular,' he said, and showed him an advertisement in the book trade weekly:

Jachin-Boaz, please contact Boaz-Jachin.

A telephone number and box number were given. Jachin-Boaz wrote them down.

'Jachin-Boaz, please contact yourself turned around,' said the bookshop owner. 'An odd message.'

'What do you mean, myself turned around?' said Jachin-Boaz.

'The names,' said the bookshop owner. 'Jachin-Boaz, Boaz-Jachin.'

'My son,' said Jachin-Boaz. 'He's not me turned around. I don't know who he is. I don't know him very well.'

'Who can know anybody?' said the bookshop owner. 'Every person is like thousands of books. New, reprinting, in stock, out of stock, fiction, non-fiction, poetry, rubbish. The lot. Different every day. One's lucky to be able to put his hand on the one that's wanted, let alone know it.'

Jachin-Boaz watched the bookshop owner walk out of the hospital looking modestly carefree and comfortable, tried to remember when he had last felt easy in his mind. Soon I'll be out of stock, he thought. All the books that I am. And out of print too, for good. Leaving a new son behind. No way back. A wave of terror flooded his being. No, no, no. Yes. No way back. Goddam her. Goddam both of them – the one he had left and the one who now stood between him and the one he had left. No going back. He didn't want to be a father again. He wasn't yet finished with being a son, and here was the last moment coming closer with every beat of his heart, that beating that he was aware of most of the time now. His heart and all the other organs in his tired body, no rest for forty-seven years. And the imminent final rest intolerable to think of. The last moment will be *now*, she had written.

He tried to find hiding places from the terror in his mind so that the letter writer and the tightly furled man would not complain of his clanging, and he avoided anyone else's company. He availed himself of as many tranquillizers as the nurses would give him, slept as much as possible, entertained himself with sex fantasies, sang songs mentally. The song that became habitual had only one word: *lion.* Lion, lion, lion, sang his mind to dance rhythms, battle tunes, lullabies.

He did not write to Boaz-Jachin or call him on the telephone. When the doctor made his rounds Jachin-Boaz spoke reasonably and cheerfully, said that the rest had done him good and that he was eager to get on with his life.

'Tockly,' said the doctor. 'There's a world of tickerence between the way you tock now and the way you ticked before, eh?'

'Yes, indeed,' said Jachin-Boaz.

'New ticksponsibilities coming up now, eh?' said the doctor. 'Tockspectant father, I hear. Best of tock, you know. Smashing young tickly you've got there. Saw her before she left.'

'Thank you,' said Jachin-Boaz.

'No more tockolence, I hope,' said the doctor. 'Won't do, you know, in her tickition.'

'Good heavens, no,' said Jachin-Boaz.

'Good boy,' said the doctor, gripping Jachin-Boaz's shoulder hard. 'That's the ticket.'

At the end of his third week in the hospital Jachin-Boaz was discharged. He watched his feet as he walked through the corridors to the front door, careful to walk like a man wearing shoes.

As he was going out he met the doctor who had treated his wounds coming in with a police constable, a social worker and a male nurse all gripping him firmly.

'Bloody wogs defiling our women,' said the doctor. 'Atheists, cultists, sexual deviants, radicals, intellectuals.'

'Cheerio,' said the nurse when he saw Jachin-Boaz. 'All the best, and don't come back too soon.'

'What's wrong with the doctor?' said Jachin-Boaz.

'Went for his wife with a poker,' said the nurse. 'She said it was the first time he'd touched her with anything stiff for a long time.'

'Whore,' said the doctor. 'She's a whore.' He stared at Jachin-Boaz. 'He's got a lion,' he said, 'and nobody does anything about it. The authorities turn a blind eye. See him smile. He's got a lion.'

# 33

When Boaz-Jachin heard the roar it came to him that there was in the world only one place. That place was time. The lion was in it and he was in it. He knew now that he must have known it when he shouted into the darkness and the ferry's white wake spreading astern. He must have known it always, from the time he had first seen the frowning face of the dying lion biting the wheel. He had made his feeble attempt at maintaining the fiction of ordinary reality, had placed the advertisement in the trade weekly. But it was towards the lion that he had been moving the emptiness in him these many miles. And it was the lion's call that he had waited for here in this city.

He put his guitar in the case, picked it up, and walked in the direction of the sound, listening past the footsteps, voices, trains and echoes. Again the roar. It came from a particular direction and seemed to be in him at the same time. No one else seemed to hear it, no one paused to listen or to look at him as if the sound were emanating from him. Listening and seeing nothing he followed through the corridors, up the stairway and the escalator to the street, smelling hot sun, dry wind and the tawny plains.

Past the traffic, past the buses, lorries, cars, footsteps, voices, aeroplanes overhead, boats on the river he listened, walking slowly. Everything that is lost is found again, he thought. The father must live so that the father can die. In him were all the faces, all the voices since he had first looked at the motionless stone in which the dying lion bit the wheel, all the skies and days, the ocean that had brought him to the time in which the lion was and he was. He walked, and in his mind he sang his wordless song.

West he followed the roar, seeing nothing, and south towards the river and its bridges. Found again, lost again, he thought. The father must live. Time flowed through him. Being was. Balanced he flowed with time and being, following the lion, his face cleaving the air, his mind singing wordlessly.

Alone among those he walked with on the streets he listened to the roar that led him on, came to the embankment. Spanned by its bridges the river flowed beneath the sky. Boaz-Jachin did not hear the roaring again. He sat down on a bench facing the river, took out his guitar and played lion-music softly.

The day faded, the moon appeared in the sky and in the river. Boaz-Jachin played his guitar, waiting.

# 34

On the morning after his first night at home Jachin-Boaz awoke without an erection. Hello, infinity, he thought. He remembered now that most of the time for the last few weeks he had not had an erection on waking. He sighed, thought of yellow leaves falling, quiet bells in monasteries, cool tombstones, poets and composers who had died young, pyramids, broken colossal statues, dry wind in the desert, grains of sand blowing, stinging, time.

Last night they had made love, and as always it had been good. Someone had felt good — he, she, it, they. Jachin-Boaz wished them all the best of luck in their new venture. The earth had to be populated with people for the aloneness to wear. Congratulations.

Gretel was still asleep. He put his hand on her belly under the blankets. One more brain to hold the world in. One more world-carrier. Like a disease the world was passed from one to the other, each to suffer alone. And yet — tiny sunrise, catch it before it's gone — the aloneness was in fact no worse than it had ever been. Even now with death coursing through him with every beat of his heart it was no worse. Secure in the womb he had been alone. The terror that was now was then as well. The terror inseparable from the primal salt, the green light through the reeds. The terror and the energy of life inseparable. Secure with his wife and son he had been alone, pulling the blankets of every day over his head to shut the terror out.

Here, anchorless and lost in this time with Gretel he was alone with the terror but no more alone than the person-to-be in her womb. Sunrise, caught. Night again. Hello, night. No darker than ever. No darker than before I was. No darker than for you in her belly before your beginning. It takes a million noes to make one yes. Who said that? I said it.

He got out of bed, stood up naked, stretched, looked at the not-yet-morning light in the window, listened to birds singing. I said I'd tell her, he thought.

He said he'd tell me, thought Gretel with her eyes closed.

He gently uncovered her, kissed her belly. I've told her, he thought.

He's told me, thought Gretel. What? She kept her eyes closed, heard Jachin-Boaz in the bathroom, heard him dressing, making coffee, going out. I don't think he bought meat, she thought. I don't think he took meat with him.

Summer, thought Jachin-Boaz. Seasons pass, the air on my face is mild, the day that is coming will be a summer day. This is better than my selfish rage in the hospital. There is no magic, nothing and no one to help me. Cool before the dawn I must do it alone, up from nothing, out of nothing. In his hand was the rolled-up master-map. Across the street stood the lion. Jachin-Boaz took from his pocket an envelope addressed to Gretel, a cheque in it payable to her for all the money in his account. He posted it in the letterbox near the telephone kiosk. The telephone kiosk was still lit. The chestnut tree, wet with morning, was in full leaf. The lion-smell hung stilly in the air.

'No meat,' said Jachin-Boaz to the lion. He turned and walked towards the river. The lion followed. As on the first day, a crow flew overhead. Jachin-Boaz came to the bridge, turned right, walked down the steps to the part of the embankment below street level. On his left were the parapet and the river, on his right the retaining wall. Behind him the steps to the bridge, ahead of him a railing at the edge of the stonework and the water stairs. The lion followed. Jachin-Boaz turned and faced him.

No magic. Reality unbearable, inescapable. Violent death. Violent life. Being beyond all reasonable bounds. Being unbounded, terrifying, violent medium of death and life, indifferent to both, contemptuous of mortal distinctions. Frowning brows. Amber eyes luminous and infinite. Open jaws, hot breath, pink rasping tongue and white teeth of the end of the world. Jachin-Boaz smelled the lion, saw him breathe, saw the breeze stir his mane, saw the muscles taut beneath the tawny skin. Immense, the lion, dominating space and time. Distinct, forward of the air around him. Immediate. Now. Nothing else.

'Lion,' said Jachin-Boaz. 'You have waited for me before the dawns. You have walked with me, have eaten my meat. You have been attentive and indifferent. You have attacked me and you have turned away. You have been seen and unseen. Here we are. Now is the only time there is.

'Life,' said Jachin-Boaz. He took one step to the left. 'Death,' he said. He stepped back to the right. 'Life,' he said, looked calmly at the lion, shrugged.

'There are no maps,' said Jachin-Boaz. He unrolled the map in his hand, rolled it the other way to flatten it, lit a match, set it afire. Flames danced up. He dropped the map as the flames consumed it, oceans and continents darkened, writhing in the fire.

'No maps,' said Jachin-Boaz.

He remembered Boaz-Jachin as a baby, laughing in his bath in the sink. He remembered his wife singing. He remembered the feel of Gretel's belly against his mouth, remembered Boaz-Jachin as a boy standing outside the shop and looking in through the window, his small mysterious face shaded by the awning. He remembered the palm trees and the fountain in the square.

'No way back,' said Jachin-Boaz.

As long before, words appeared in his mind, large, powerful, compelling belief and respect like the saying of a god in capital letters:

### TO SING IN THE PRESENCE OF A LION

Jachin-Boaz looked into the eyes of the lion. Someone was coming down the steps from the bridge with a guitar, was playing the guitar, was playing lion-music.

Jachin-Boaz was not trembling. His voice was firm. He was surprised at how strong his voice was, how pleasing. He sang:

> Lion, lion, ten thousand years,
> Ten thousand more and still
> The motion of your running,
> Tawny, great, the motion of your running
> Printed on the air.
> The earth upon your amber eyes, lion,
> Ten thousand years, ten thousand more.
> Dead the kings are, lion,
> Fleshed with earth their bones,
> The earth upon your amber eyes,
> Like a window you looked through it, lion.
> The wheel you died on turns, you rise.
> The river and the bridges, lion,
> Crossings always, birds of morning,
> The motion of your running,
> Tawny, great upon the air.

The air was dense and shimmering, thick with time. The taste of salt was in the mouth of Jachin-Boaz, Boaz-Jachin. Ocean behind him, the father saw the lion through the green light in the reeds, ceased to be himself, and only was. A channel through which life surged up, returned again to earth, to ocean. Immense in him a million rising noes to make one yes. No words. No *no* great enough. Jachin-Boaz opened his mouth, Boaz-Jachin opened his mouth.

The sound filled all space like a river in flood, a great river of lion-coloured sound. From his time, from the tawny running on the plains, from the pit and the fall and the oblong of blue sky overhead, from his death on the spears in the dry wind forward into all the darknesses and lights revolving to the morning light above the city and the river with its bridges the lion, father, son sent his roar.

'Right,' said the police constable on the bridge, speaking into the little two-way radio he held. 'Right. I am standing at the north end of the bridge. I am facing west, looking down the steps. There are two men there with a lion. Right. I know. The lion is loose. I am dead sober. I am in my right mind. What I think we need here is the fire brigade with a pumper. Big net too, stout one. Chaps from the zoo with a strong cage. Ambulance too. Yes, I know this is the second time. As quick as you can.' The constable looked up and down the bridge, chose a position from which he could climb a lamp-post or jump into the river, and waited.

More, thought Jachin-Boaz. This is not yet all. I have not yet gone all the way. I have not yet become unaware of the beating of my heart, have not yet eaten up my terror, not yet been angry enough. Let it come, let it happen. Words in his mind again:

TO RAGE WITH A LION

Nothing else was enough. No more thought. His mouth opened. Again the roar. He or the lion? He smelled the lion. Life, death. He hurled himself at the immensity of lion.

Boaz-Jachin leaped from the other side on to the lion's back, his face against the coarse mane and hot tawny skin, his arms embracing, fingers clutching raging death.

Jachin-Boaz, Boaz-Jachin screamed in blinding fires of pain, raw nerves and ripped flesh flaming, muscles torn, ribs cracking, lion-entered, lion-killed, lion-born, howling in millennia of pain, impossibly absorbing infinities of lion. Blackness. Light. Silence.

Their arms were around each other. They were whole, unhurt. There was no great beast between them. The day was bright on the river, the air was warm. They nodded to each other, shook their heads, kissed, laughed, cried, cursed.

'You're taller,' said Jachin-Boaz.

'You're looking well,' said Boaz-Jachin. He picked up his guitar, put it in the case. They walked up the steps, turned down the street towards Jachin-Boaz's flat. The fire brigade pumper and a red car passed them flashing and blaring. The ambulance, a police car, a police van, a van from the zoo, all flashing and blaring.

'You'll have breakfast with us,' said Jachin-Boaz. 'I don't mind being a little late for work today.'

The police constable came forward as the pumper, the ambulance, the cars and vans screeched to a stop. In a moment he was the centre of a circle of policemen, firemen, ambulance and zoo people, and his superintendent. The little dark man from the zoo sniffed the air, looked from side to side, bent to study the pavement.

The superintendent looked at the constable, shook his head. 'Not twice, Phillips,' he said.

'I know how it looks, sir,' said the constable.

'You've got a good record, Phillips,' said the superintendent. 'Good prospects for promotion, a fine career ahead of you. Sometimes things get to be too much for all of us. Marital problems, economic pressures, nervous strain, all kinds of worries. I want you to talk to a doctor.'

'No,' said the constable. He put the two-way radio carefully on the bridge parapet.

'No,' he said again. He took off his helmet, set it down beside the radio.

'No,' he said once more, took off his tunic, folded it neatly, laid it on the parapet beside the helmet and radio.

'There *was* a lion,' he said. 'There is a lion. Lion is.'

He nodded to the superintendent, passed through the circle as it parted on either side of him, and walked away down the street in his shirtsleeves.